ROWAN DUNCAN

ALBATROSS

or, The Sea of Madness

First published by Snakebite Press Publishing 2024

Copyright © 2024 by Rowan Duncan

All rights reserved. No part of this publication may be reproduced, stored or transmitted in any form or by any means, electronic, mechanical, photocopying, recording, scanning, or otherwise without written permission from the publisher. It is illegal to copy this book, post it to a website, or distribute it by any other means without permission.

This novel is entirely a work of fiction. The names, characters and incidents portrayed in it are the work of the author's imagination. Any resemblance to actual persons, living or dead, events or localities is entirely coincidental.

Rowan Duncan asserts the moral right to be identified as the author of this work.

Designations used by companies to distinguish their products are often claimed as trademarks. All brand names and product names used in this book and on its cover are trade names, service marks, trademarks and registered trademarks of their respective owners. The publishers and the book are not associated with any product or vendor mentioned in this book. None of the companies referenced within the book have endorsed the book.

"Moby Dick or The Whale" by Herman Melville © 1851 (Public Domain)

First edition

ISBN: 9781088194959

Cover art by Donn Warnauc

This book was professionally typeset on Reedsy. Find out more at reedsy.com

For
My Family,
Biological and Otherwise...

At times we gasped for breath at an elevation beyond the Albatross—-at times became dizzy with the velocity of our descent into some watery hell, where the air grew stagnant, and no sound disturbed the slumbers of the Kraken.

- Edgar Allan Poe, 1833

…what evil looks had I from old and young! Instead of the cross, the Albatross about my neck was hung.

- Samuel Taylor Coleridge, 1798

Publisher's Statement

A Note on Mental Health...

Mental health conditions affect millions of people worldwide, touching every community, culture, and profession. While this work of fiction explores themes of psychological deterioration and violence, it is crucial to understand that mental health challenges and violence are not inherently linked. The vast majority of individuals living with mental health conditions are not violent, and are in fact more likely to be victims of violence than perpetrators.

This novel is a work of psychological fiction that examines the complex interplay of personal choices, professional burnout, and moral deterioration. It should not be read as representative of mental health professionals, who perform vital and challenging work helping millions of people lead healthier, more fulfilled lives. Psychiatrists, psychologists, and other mental health practitioners undergo rigorous training and adhere to strict ethical guidelines while providing essential care to their communities.

For those struggling with mental health challenges, please know that help is available. Mental health conditions are treatable, and recovery is possible with proper support and care. If you or someone you know is experiencing mental health difficulties, we encourage you to reach out to qualified mental health professionals who can provide appropriate care and guidance.

The publishing team acknowledges the sensitivity of the themes explored in this work and encourages readers to approach the narrative with the understanding that it represents a fictional exploration of individual moral choices rather than a commentary on mental illness or the mental health profession as a whole.

Resources for Support:

- National Crisis Hotline: Available 24/7
- National Alliance on Mental Illness (NAMI): Offering education, support groups, and advocacy
- Mental Health America: Providing screening tools and educational resources
- American Psychiatric Association: Information on mental health conditions and treatment options
- Local mental health clinics and community health centers

We believe that open dialogue about mental health helps reduce stigma and encourages those in need to seek help. However, such discussions must be approached with sensitivity, understanding, and respect for those affected by mental health challenges.

The characters and events in this novel are entirely fictional. Any resemblance to real persons, living or deceased, or actual events, is purely coincidental. The views and actions of the characters do not reflect the views of the publisher, author, or mental health community.

We are committed to promoting responsible discussion of mental health issues and supporting initiatives that advance understanding, treatment, and support for those affected by mental health conditions.

For more information about mental health resources and support services in your area, please consult with healthcare providers or visit reputable mental health organizations online.

Remember: Mental health conditions are medical conditions, deserving of the same compassion, understanding, and professional treatment as any physical ailment. Recovery is possible, and help is available.

Prologue

The U.S. Coast Guard cutter sliced through the crystal-clear cyan waters off the coast of St. Croix, as the Caribbean sun beat down on its deck. Officer Allison Quint stood at the bow, her dark eyes scanning the horizon. The salt-laden breeze whipped her short, pixie-cut hair as she searched for any sign of the missing vessel.

"There!" she called out, pointing to a dark shape bobbing in the distance.

As they drew closer, the shape materialized into the half-submerged hull of a boat. Its cream-colored deck was barely visible above the waterline, and the burgundy and black paint along its sides glistened in the sunlight.

"That's gotta be the Harbinger," Allison muttered, recognizing the vessel from the description in the *Mayday-Lost at sea* report.

The cutter slowed to a stop, and Allison led the boarding party onto the listing deck of the abandoned trawler. Water sloshed around their ankles as they made their way towards the cabin.

She had joined the Coast Guard five years ago, drawn by a desire to protect and serve on the open waters she'd grown to love during her childhood in coastal Maine. The thrill of search and rescue missions had kept her passion alive, but it was the investigative side of her job that truly fired her up.

As she stepped into the waterlogged cabin, her trained eye took in every detail. Overturned furniture, broken glass, and scattered personal belongings told a story of violence – whether from a storm or something more sinister, she couldn't yet tell.

A leather-bound book caught her attention, floating near the helm. She fished it out of the water, recognizing it as a journal. The name "Dr. Pete Corbin" was scrawled on the inside cover.

"Bag this and any other personal effects," she ordered her team. "And check for any sign of blood or foul play."

Back on the cutter, she sat in her small office, the rescued journal on the desk before her. She hesitated for a moment, knowing that reading it might be a breach of privacy. But if the missing doctor was still alive out there, every moment counted.

She opened the journal, its pages warped and stained from seawater. The first entry was dated three weeks ago:

May 15th - I can't take it anymore. The guilt, the lies, they're eating me alive. Jenny suspects something, I can see it in her eyes. And Amy... God, what have I done? I need to get away, clear my head. Maybe out there on the water, I can find some peace.

Allison frowned, sensing the turmoil in Dr. Corbin's words. She flipped through the pages, skimming entries that detailed his preparations for a fishing trip.

The next few entries described hiss fishing expeditions and his attempts to relax.

She pulled out her phone and dialed her supervisor.

"Sir, I think we need to expand our search area. And I'm going to need everything we have on Dr. Pete Corbin."

With an unsettling feeling, she turned back to the journal. Whatever had happened to Pete Corbin, she was determined to uncover the truth. Even if it meant diving into the depths of a mystery as vast and unpredictable as the Caribbean Sea itself.

.

.

One

Men are not punished for their sins, but by them.
— *Elbert Hubbard*

Pete Corbin hefted a cooler into the back of his pickup truck, his muscles straining under the weight. He paused, wiping sweat from his brow, and gazed out at Frederiksted Harbor. The water stretched out into the Caribbean Sea before him, a promise of escape from the troubles that plagued him on land.

He turned back to his supplies, methodically checking off items on a mental list. Fishing rods, tackle boxes, emergency flares. His hands brushed against the leather-bound journal tucked into his duffel bag. He pulled it out, running his fingers over the embossed cover. The crisp, blank pages inside waited to be filled with the story of his adventure.

As he loaded the last of his gear, his mind drifted. The weight of recent events pressed down on him, threatening to crush his spirit. He shook his head, trying to clear the fog of guilt and regret that clouded his thoughts.

The slam of the truck's tailgate echoed across the quiet neighborhood. He climbed into the driver's seat, his movements automatic. He sat there for a moment, hands gripping the steering wheel.

A memory surfaced, uninvited and unwelcome.

The sun baked the rickety dock, its weathered planks creaking under their feet. Pete, barely twelve years old, clutched a fishing rod in sweaty hands. His father, Jonathon, stood beside him, a giant of a man with calloused hands and a perpetual frown.

"You're holding it wrong," Jonathon growled, snatching the rod from Pete's grasp. "How many times do I have to show you?"

Pete flinched, shrinking away from his father's anger.

"Sorry, Dad. I'm trying."

Jonathon's eyes narrowed, disappointment etched in every line of his face.

"Trying isn't good enough, boy. You need to do better."

He demonstrated the proper technique, his movements fluid and practiced. Pete watched, desperately trying to memorize every detail. When Jonathon handed the rod back, Pete's hands shook.

"Now cast," Jonathon ordered, crossing his arms over his broad chest.

Pete took a breath, willing his nerves to steady. He drew the rod back, then whipped it forward with all his might. The line sailed through the air, arcing gracefully over the water. For a moment, hope bloomed in his chest.

Then the hook caught on the back of his shirt, yanking him off balance. He stumbled, arms pinwheeling, and toppled off the dock with a yelp. He hit the water with a splash, sinking beneath the surface.

Panic gripped him as he flailed, struggling to find his way back up. Just as his lungs began to burn, a strong hand plunged into the water and hauled him to the surface. He gasped for air, coughing and sputtering.

Jonathon dragged him back onto the dock, a look of fury and disgust on his face.

"Can't you do anything right?"

Pete huddled on the dock, soaking wet and shivering. Tears stung his eyes, but he blinked them back. Crying would only make things worse.

"I'm sorry," he whispered.

Jonathon shook his head, turning away.

"Hopeless. I don't ever want to hear another word about fishing coming from you. Understand? Never again."

The words cut deeper than any hook, leaving wounds that would never fully heal. He wanted to learn to fish and he knew his grandfather would happily teach him, but it wasn't the same. He longed for that connection with his father.

The event left him with a life-long fear of drowning, despite his eventual passion for the sea and learning to be an expert swimmer.

He blinked, the memory fading. He found himself still sitting in his truck, the engine idling. The clock on the dashboard showed that nearly an hour had passed while he'd been lost in thought.

***

He sat in his truck, the engine idling softly in the pre-dawn darkness. His thumb twiddled with the wedding ring on the same hand as he stared at his phone. The screen glowed, illuminating Jennifer's name and number. He took a deep breath and hit the call button.

The phone rang once, twice, three times before Jennifer's crisp voice cut through the silence.

"Pete? It's five in the morning. What's going on?"

"Hey, Jen. I'm… I'm heading out for that fishing trip I mentioned."

A pause hung between them, stretching into uncomfortable territory before Jennifer spoke again.

"The one you *mentioned* last night at dinner? The trip you decided on without any discussion?"

Pete winced. He could picture her face, eyes narrowed, lips pressed into a thin line.

"Look, I know it's sudden, but—"

"Sudden?" Jennifer's voice rose slightly. "Pete, you have patients scheduled all week. What am I supposed to tell them? That their psychiatrist decided to go fishing on a whim?"

Pete's grip tightened on the steering wheel.

"It's not a whim. I need this, Jen. I've been feeling… off lately. The stress—"

"And running away to the ocean is your solution? What about your responsibilities? What about us?"

The last word hung in the air, heavy with unspoken accusations. Pete closed his eyes, fighting back a wave of guilt.

"It's just for a week. I'll reschedule my appointments. You can handle the practice for a few days, can't you?"

"That's not the point, Pete. We're supposed to be partners. You can't just make decisions like this without talking to me first."

Pete's free hand clenched into a fist. He wanted to explain, to make her understand the restlessness that had been gnawing at him for weeks. But the words wouldn't come. Instead, he said, "I left some notes on the kitchen counter about the appointments. There's a list of patients who might need extra attention."

Jennifer sighed, a sound that seemed to carry the weight of a thousand unresolved arguments.

"Always the doctor, aren't you? Even when you're running away."

"I'm not running away," He snapped, his temper flaring. "I just need some time to clear my head. Is that so hard to understand?"

"What I understand," Jennifer said, her voice now cool and controlled, "is that when things get tough, you check out. You did it after your father's funeral, and you're doing it now."

Pete felt as if he'd been slapped. The mention of his father sent a jolt of pain through him, reopening old wounds.

"That's not fair, Jen. You know how complicated things were with my dad."

"And things aren't complicated now?" she said.

Images of Amy flashed through Pete's thoughts. He pushed them away, guilt churning in his stomach.

"I just need some time alone. To think. To figure things out."

"Figure what out, Pete?" Jennifer's voice was almost sad now. "What aren't you telling me?"

The silence was filled with unspoken truths and half-formed confessions. Pete's throat felt tight, his mouth dry.

"Nothing. There's nothing to tell. I just... I need this trip."

Jennifer was quiet for a long moment. When she spoke again, her voice was resigned.

"Fine. Go on your damn trip. But when you get back, we need to talk. Really talk, Pete. About us, about where we're headed."

He nodded, forgetting for a moment that she couldn't see him.

"Yeah. Okay. We'll talk when I get back."

"Be careful out there," Jennifer said, her practical nature asserting itself even now. "Did you check the weather reports? Make sure you have enough supplies?"

Despite everything, he felt a small smile tug at his lips.

"Yes, dear. I've got everything I need. I'll be fine."

"You'd better be," she said, a hint of her usual dry humor creeping into her voice. "I don't want to have to explain to your patients why their therapist got lost at sea."

Pete's smile faded as quickly as it had appeared.

"I'll be careful. I promise."

"Alright then," she said. "Guess... I'll see you in a week."

"Yeah. A week," he said.

He hesitated, words of love and apology on the tip of his tongue. But before he could speak, the line went dead.

He stared at the phone in his hand, the screen fading to black. The silence in the truck felt oppressive, filled with the echoes of their conversation and the weight of everything left unsaid. He tossed the phone onto the passenger seat and put the truck in gear, pulling away from the curb.

As he drove down the road, he couldn't shake the feeling that he was leaving more than just his home behind. With each mile that passed, the distance between him and Jennifer seemed to grow, stretching into an uncrossable chasm.

* * *

Pete's truck rumbled to a stop outside Amy's modest bungalow. The sun-bleached paint peeled from the wooden siding, and overgrown bougainvillea spilled onto the cracked sidewalk. He killed the engine and sat for a moment, his fingers drumming an erratic rhythm on the steering wheel.

The front door swung open before he reached the porch. Amy stood there, back-lit by the warm glow of her living room. Her blonde hair tumbled in messy waves around her shoulders, and her green eyes sparkled with a mix of excitement and something darker.

"I was starting to think you weren't coming," she said, her voice a husky whisper.

He stepped inside, the familiar scent of sandalwood incense and Amy's perfume washing over him.

"Had to finish packing," he muttered, avoiding her gaze.

Amy's fingers trailed along his arm, leaving goosebumps in their

ONE

wake.

"You're really going through with it, huh? A whole week *alone* on that boat of yours?"

He nodded, finally meeting her eyes.

"I need this, Amy."

She pulled away abruptly, pacing the small living room. Colorful tapestries adorned the walls, and crystals caught the light from mismatched lamps. A collection of worn throw pillows covered a secondhand leather couch, their tassels trailing on the hardwood floor. Wind chimes tinkled softly by the open window. Empty wine bottles lined the windowsill, each one holding a half-burned candle, dried wax dripping down their sides like frozen tears.

"And where does that leave us?" she said, a bitter edge to her words.

Pete sighed, sinking onto the worn leather couch.

"It's complicated."

Amy whirled to face him, her eyes flashing.

"It's always complicated with you, Pete. When are you going to make a decision?"

He ran a hand through his hair, frustration bubbling up.

"You know it's not that simple... Jennifer, my practice—"

"Your precious reputation," Amy cut in, her voice dripping with sarcasm.

She moved closer, straddling his lap in one fluid motion. Her fingers traced the line of his jaw.

"What about what you want, Pete? What about us?"

The heat of her body against his was intoxicating. His resolve wavered, his hands instinctively settling on her hips.

"Amy, I—"

She silenced him with a kiss, fierce and demanding. He responded despite himself, losing himself in the familiar dance of lips and tongues. When they broke apart, both were breathing heavily.

"Tell me you don't feel anything," Amy said, her eyes searching his face.

He closed his eyes, fighting the war raging inside him.

"You know I care about you," he said softly.

Amy climbed off his lap, her movements sharp and angry.

"Care about me? That's rich."

She walked into the kitchen, returning with a bottle of tequila and two shot glasses.

"If you're leaving me for a week, the least you can do is have a drink with me."

He eyed the bottle warily.

"Amy, I shouldn't. I need to get to the marina—"

She slammed the glasses down on the coffee table.

"One drink, He. For old times' sake."

Against his better judgment, he nodded. Amy poured two generous shots, her hands steady despite the storm of emotions playing across her face. She handed him a glass, raising her own in a mock toast.

"To complicated relationships," she said, her voice laced with bitterness.

They clinked glasses and downed the shots. The tequila burned his throat, settling like liquid fire in his stomach. Amy was already pouring another round.

"Amy, I really should go."

She ignored him, pressing the second shot into his hand.

"Tell me about the boat trip. Where are you planning to go?"

He took a small sip, trying to pace himself.

"Just out into the Caribbean. No real destination in mind."

Amy's eyes lit up with a dangerous glint.

"Sounds romantic. Room for two on that boat of yours?"

He shook his head, setting the glass down.

"It's not that kind of trip. I need time to think."

ONE

"To think," Amy said, downing her shot. "Always thinking, never doing."

She moved closer, her fingers playing with the buttons of his shirt.

"What if I gave you something else to think about?"

He caught her wrist, gently but firmly.

"Amy, we can't. Not now."

Hurt flashed across her face, quickly replaced by anger. She yanked her hand away.

"Fine. Go on your little soul-searching voyage. But don't expect me to be waiting when you get back."

He stood, desperate to escape the suffocating tension of the room.

"Amy, I'm sorry—"

"Save it," she said, turning her back on him. "Go. But just know, STX is a big island, but it's still just an island."

"What does that mean?" Pete said.

"I'm just saying, If I happen to run into your wife at the market or someplace..."

"C'mon, Amy. Don't be that way. You're not gonna say a thing to Jennifer. We've discussed this. It would destroy her. Has to be handled slowly and delicately."

He hesitated, wanting to say more but knowing it would only make things worse. He moved towards the door, pausing with his hand on the knob.

"I'll call ya when I get back. Won't be any cell service out there."

Amy's shoulders stiffened, but she didn't turn around.

"Don't bother."

The door clicked shut behind him, leaving him standing on the porch, the warm Caribbean breeze doing nothing to cool the turmoil inside him. He walked to his truck on unsteady legs, the tequila and guilt a potent combination.

As he drove towards the marina, he couldn't shake the image of

Amy's face—hurt, angry, and something else he couldn't quite place. He gripped the steering wheel tighter, trying to focus on the road ahead and not the mess he was leaving behind.

* * *

Pete's boots thudded against the wooden planks of the dock as he approached his forty-three foot trawler, the *Harbinger*. The marina bustled with activity, fishermen and pleasure-seekers alike preparing for a day on the water. The smell of salt and diesel hung in the air, mingling with the cries of seagulls overhead.

He paused at the stern, running his hand along the smooth burgundy hull. The cream-colored deck gleamed in the early morning sunlight, a contrast to the dark thoughts swirling in his mind. He breathed deep, savoring the crisp sea air that filled his lungs.

As he stepped aboard, the boat rocked gently beneath his feet. The familiar motion brought a small smile to his face, a brief respite from the weight of his troubles. He made his way to the wheelhouse, his fingers trailing along the polished teak railings.

Inside, he stowed his duffel bag and supplies in their designated spots. Everything had its place on the Harbinger. He pulled out his journal, running his thumb over the worn leather cover before tucking it into a drawer near the helm.

The boat's engine rumbled to life with a turn of the key, the vibrations thrumming through the deck. He felt a surge of excitement course through him. Out here, he was the master of his own destiny. No disappointed wife… no demanding mistress. Just him, the sea, and the promise of adventure.

ONE

He cast off the mooring lines and eased the Harbinger out of its slip. As the boat glided past the breakwater, he felt the tension in his shoulders begin to loosen.

Yet, as the shoreline receded behind him, a nagging unease settled in the pit of his stomach. He gripped the wheel tighter, his knuckles whitening. The freedom he sought felt overwhelming, almost suffocating.

He shook his head, trying to dispel the feeling. He focused on the horizon, on the gentle rise and fall of the waves. This was what he needed – time alone to clear his head, to figure out how to untangle the mess he'd made of his life.

The sun climbed higher in the sky as the Harbinger cut through the water. He settled into the rhythm of the journey, checking his instruments and making minor course corrections. He kept his eyes peeled for any signs of fish, eager to drop his lines.

As the morning wore on, the unease returned, stronger this time. He found himself glancing over his shoulder, half-expecting to see someone – or something – following him. But there was nothing, just the wake of his boat stretching back towards the distant shore.

He tried to rationalize his feelings. It was just nerves, the natural apprehension of being alone on the open sea. But a part of him wondered if it was something more. Was it guilt gnawing at him? Fear of the consequences of his actions?

His thoughts drifted to Jennifer, her face etched with disappointment during their last conversation. Then to Amy, her green eyes flashing with passion and frustration. And finally, to his father, Jonathon, whose stern disapproval seemed to follow Pete even in death.

This trip was supposed to be an escape, a chance to leave all that behind. But it seemed his demons had followed him, stowing away on the Harbinger like unwelcome passengers.

As the sun reached its zenith, he spotted a promising area for fishing.

He slowed the boat, preparing to drop anchor. The routine of readying his gear provided a friendly distraction from his troubled thoughts.

He baited his hooks. The familiar motions soothed his frayed nerves. As he cast his line into the water, he felt a glimmer of the peace he'd been seeking. The gentle lapping of waves against the hull and the occasional cry of a distant seabird were the only sounds that broke the silence.

Yet, as he settled in to wait for a bite, the unease returned.

This was ridiculous. He was a grown man, an experienced sailor.

As the afternoon wore on, his discomfort grew. The fish weren't biting, and the sun beating down on the deck felt more punishing than pleasant.

He reeled in his lines, deciding to move to a new spot. As he raised the anchor, a shadow passed overhead. He looked up, squinting against the sun. He thought it might be a plane, but there was no sound.

He blinked and looked. There was nothing there but clear blue sky. He rubbed his eyes, chalking it up to fatigue and the glare off the water.

Two

Pete reached for his journal, its leather cover worn smooth from years of use. He flipped it open to a fresh page and began to write:

May 18th.
Finally escaped the suffocating grip of land. The open sea stretches before me, endless and full of promise. No more pretending, no more lies. Out here, I'm just a man and his boat. The sea doesn't judge. It doesn't demand explanations or apologies. It simply is. Maybe out here, I can finally be myself without fear or shame.
There's a purity to fishing that I've never found anywhere else. Just man against nature, wits against instinct. No room for doubt or second-guessing. When I'm out here with my rod in hand, everything else falls away. I wonder sometimes if I was born in the wrong era. Maybe I should have been a sailor in the age of exploration, charting unknown waters and discovering new lands. There's something in me that craves that kind of freedom, that kind of purpose.
Out here, I'm not Dr. Pete Corbin, successful psychiatrist with a screwed up personal life. I'm just Pete, a man who loves the sea and knows how to catch fish. It's simpler. Easier. I don't have to pretend to be someone I'm not. I've always felt a connection to the sea that I can't quite explain. It's like coming home, in a way. The vastness of it, the power – it puts everything

into perspective. My problems seem small and insignificant out here.

The night is coming on. I'll drop anchor here, fish a bit in the morning. Out here, under the stars, I can breathe. I can think. Maybe I'll finally figure out what I really want, who I really am. For now, though, it's enough to simply be.

He closed his journal, tucking it safely away in the cabin. He moved to the bow of the boat, leaning against the railing as he watched the last rays of sunlight fade from the sky. The sea stretched out before him, dark and mysterious, full of possibilities. Whatever tomorrow might bring, tonight he was exactly where he needed to be.

* * *

Pete fixed his eyes on the horizon where the sea met the sky in a seamless navy blue. The gentle rocking of the boat and the salty breeze should have brought him peace, but his mind churned with memories he couldn't shake.

His thoughts dragged him back to a recent evening in Frederiksted.

He and Jennifer sat at their kitchen table, the remains of dinner pushed aside. The air between them crackled with tension. Jennifer's fingers tapped an impatient rhythm on her water glass, her hazel eyes sharp and unyielding.

"Another fishing trip, Pete? Really?"

"I need this, Jen. You know how work's been lately."

Jennifer's eyebrow arched.

"Work? Or is it *something else*?"

His stomach clenched. He forced himself to meet her gaze, willing his face to remain neutral.

"What's that supposed to mean?"

She leaned back in her chair, crossing her arms.

"You've been distant. Distracted. I'm not blind, Pete."

The words were heavy with implication between them. Pete's mind searched for a response that wouldn't betray him.

"It's just stress. The job, you know how it is."

Jennifer's laugh was short and bitter.

"The job. Right. Because being a successful psychiatrist is so grueling."

He felt a flare of anger.

"You have no idea what it's like, listening to people's problems day in and day out. It takes a toll."

"And what about our problems, Pete? When do we address those?"

He stood abruptly, his chair scraping against the floor.

Jennifer rose to meet him, her eyes flashing.

"You always say you're just going out to *clear your head*. Clear your head of what? Of me? Of us?"

He turned away, unable to face the hurt in her eyes. He moved to the sink, gripping the edge.

"That's not fair, Jen."

"Fair?" She laughed again, the sound harsh in the quiet kitchen. "What's not fair is feeling like I'm losing my husband and not knowing why."

Pete's shoulders tensed. He wanted to tell her she was wrong, that nothing had changed. But the lie stuck in his throat.

Jennifer's voice softened, tinged with a sadness that cut deeper than her anger. "We used to talk, Pete. About everything. When did that stop?"

He turned to face her, seeing the woman he'd fallen in love with all those years ago. The woman he'd vowed to cherish and protect. The woman he'd betrayed.

"I'm sorry," he said, the words inadequate even as they left his mouth. "I don't mean to shut you out."

Jennifer stepped closer, her hand reaching for his.

"Then don't. Talk to me. Tell me what's going on in that head of yours."

For a moment, he considered confessing everything. The guilt, the fear, the terrible secret that weighed on him. But as he looked into Jennifer's eyes, he couldn't bear the thought of destroying her world.

Instead, he pulled her into an embrace, burying his face in her hair.

"I love you," he whispered, hoping she couldn't hear the desperation in his voice.

Jennifer's arms tightened around him.

"I love you too. But love isn't enough if we're not honest with each other."

He pulled back, cupping her face in his hands.

"When I get back, we'll talk. I promise. I just need this time to sort things out."

Jennifer searched his face, her expression a mix of hope and doubt.

"Okay," she said finally. "But this is the last time, Pete. No more running."

He nodded, sealing the promise with a kiss that tasted of regret and unspoken truths. That was two fishing trips ago. It was always the same story.

* * *

Pete's fingers grazed the cool metal of the flask, hidden beneath a stack of energy bars in his supply crate. He pulled it out, squinting as he looked at it. The weight felt familiar in his hand, but he had no recollection of packing it.

The Harbinger rocked gently on the calm sea as he turned the flask over in his palm. Moonlight glinted off its surface, revealing a series of small scratches along the bottom edge. He unscrewed the cap and took a cautious sniff. The sharp scent of tequila hit his nostrils, triggering a wave of conflicting emotions.

Tequila? He thought.

He set the flask on the galley counter and ran a hand through his salt-stiffened hair. He tried to piece together how it had found its way onto his boat.

As he moved to return the flask to the crate, a folded piece of paper fluttered to the floor. He froze, staring at it for a long moment before bending to pick it up. The paper was thick and cream-colored, nothing like the paper in his journal.

With trembling fingers, he unfolded the note. The handwriting was unfamiliar – a looping, feminine script that flowed across the page in dark blue ink. His eyes darted over the words, his confusion deepening with each line:

The sea holds secrets, Pete. Some are meant to stay buried. Others will claw their way to the surface, no matter how deep you try to sink them. Choose wisely.

Pete read the note three times, his heart pounding harder with each pass. He searched his memory for any clue about its origin, but came up empty. The words seemed to mock him, hinting at knowledge he didn't possess.

He glanced at the flask, then back at the note. A chill ran down his spine despite the warm night air. His gaze darted around the cabin, feeling exposed. The darkness beyond the windows seemed to press in, watching, waiting.

His hand reached for the flask without conscious thought. The liquor burned as it hit the back of his throat, but he welcomed the sensation. It grounded him, pulling him back from the edge of panic that had begun to creep in.

As the alcohol warmed his insides, his mind whirled.

He took another swig from the flask, larger this time. The boat's gentle rocking felt more pronounced, and he steadied himself against the counter. His eyes fell on his journal, lying open on the small table where he'd left it earlier.

He stumbled over, tequila sloshing in the flask as he moved. He flipped through the pages, searching for any similarity in the handwriting. His own messy scrawl stared back at him, nothing at all like the elegant script on the note.

The boat lurched unexpectedly, sending him stumbling. He caught himself on the edge of the table, knocking his journal to the floor. As he bent to retrieve it, a flash of movement outside the window caught his eye.

His head snapped up, searching the darkness. For a split second, he could have sworn he saw a face peering in at him – pale and distorted, with eyes that gleamed in the moonlight. He blinked, and it was gone.

Heart racing, he scrambled to his feet. He pressed his face against the glass, straining to see into the night. The sea was black and empty. No sign of another boat, no explanation for what he'd seen – or thought he'd seen.

His grip tightened on the flask as he backed away from the window. He tried to make sense of the situation. The note's words echoed in his head, taking on a more sinister tone with each repetition.

He fumbled for the light switch, flooding the cabin with harsh fluorescent light. The sudden brightness made him squint, but he felt a small measure of relief as the shadows retreated. His eyes darted around the familiar space, searching for anything out of place.

Everything looked normal, yet wrong somehow. The air felt thick,

TWO

charged with an energy he couldn't explain. His gaze fell on his reflection in the small mirror above the sink. His face was pale, eyes wide and slightly unfocused.

The flask slipped from his grasp, clattering to the floor. Tequila pooled around his feet, but he made no move to clean it up. He stood frozen, staring at his reflection as the boat rocked beneath him.

* * *

Pete leaned against the railing of the Harbinger, his eyes on the stars above. He breathed in, inhaling the salty sea air.

The night sky was endless, a curtain of deep, dark blue, almost black, dotted with countless pinpricks of light. The Milky Way arched across the heavens, a misty river of stars that seemed close enough to touch. He marveled at the clarity of the view, free from the light pollution civilization.

As he gazed upward, memories of his childhood surfaced. He remembered lying on the grass in their backyard, his father pointing out constellations with calloused hands. Jonathon's gruff voice softened as he spoke of ancient myths and celestial navigation.

"See that bright star there, Pete? That's Polaris, the North Star. Sailors have used it to find their way for centuries."

Pete's eyes sought out Polaris now, finding comfort in its steadfast presence. He wondered if his father had ever looked at the same star and thought of him.

The memory shifted, and he found himself recalling a camping trip when he was twelve. They'd camped out in some woods in Texas, far from the city lights. As night fell, his father had beckoned him out of the tent.

"Come on, boy. I want to show you something."

They'd stood side by side, necks craned back, as a meteor shower painted streaks of light across the sky. Pete had gasped in wonder, and for a moment, he'd felt a connection with his father that transcended their usual tension.

"Make a wish, Pete," Jonathon had said, his voice uncharacteristically gentle. "Nights like these don't come often."

Pete closed his eyes, remembering the wish he'd made that night. He'd wished for his father's approval, for a sign that he was good enough. Now, decades later, he wondered if that wish had ever come true.

The sound of water slapping against the hull brought Pete back to the present. He opened his eyes, blinking away the moisture that had gathered there. The stars above seemed to blur and shift, and for a moment, he thought he saw patterns forming in the sky – accusatory faces, pointing fingers.

He shook his head, trying to clear the unsettling images. He focused on the constellations he remembered from his youth. Orion's belt glimmered, three perfect points in a row. The Big Dipper hung low on the horizon, its handle pointing towards the North Star.

As he traced the familiar shapes, he began to question the choices that had led him to this moment. What would his father think of him now? A successful psychiatrist on the surface, but beneath that veneer, a man running from his responsibilities, his guilt.

The stars seemed to pulse with an otherworldly light, and he felt a wave of vertigo wash over him. He gripped the railing tighter, steadying himself. The vast emptiness of the sea and sky pressed in around him, making him feel small and insignificant.

In that moment of vulnerability, he longed for the simplicity of those childhood nights. He yearned for the quiet companionship he'd shared with his father, even if it had been fleeting. Despite their differences, despite the harsh words and disappointments that had come later, those moments under the stars held a purity that he desperately missed.

He thought of Jennifer, her practical nature a contrast to the whimsical beauty of the night sky. Would she understand this feeling of awe and longing? Or would she dismiss it as another of his flights of fancy?

And then there was Amy, passionate and impulsive. She'd probably love this view, would likely insist on dancing beneath the stars. But even that thought brought a pang of guilt rather than joy.

His gaze drifted back to Polaris, steady and unwavering. He wondered if it was possible to find his way back – not just to shore, but to some version of himself that he could be proud of. The weight of his choices pressed down on him, heavier than the endless sky above.

A cool breeze ruffled his hair, carrying with it the faint scent of rain. He looked to the horizon, searching for signs of an approaching storm, but saw only stars meeting sea in an unbroken line.

He pushed himself away from the railing, restless. He paced the deck, his footsteps echoing in the quiet night.

He paused, looking back at the sky one last time. The stars winked down at him, silent witnesses to his inner turmoil.

But the stars offered no solutions, no absolution. They simply shone on, indifferent to the struggles of one man alone on a dark sea. He turned away, heading back to the cabin, leaving the night sky behind him.

Three

Pete stirred as the first rays of sunlight crept through the cabin window, casting his face in a warm glow. He blinked, disoriented for a moment, before remembering where he was. He sat up, stretching his arms above his head and feeling the satisfying pop of his joints. The previous night's uneasiness had melted away, replaced by a sense of calm that settled deep in his bones. He swung his legs over the side of the bunk and walked barefoot to the deck.

The sight that greeted him took his breath away. The sun hung low on the horizon, a brilliant orb of orange and gold that painted the sky in vibrant hues. The sea was a shimmering blue that seemed to go on forever.

He made his way to the bow of the boat, gripping the railing as he leaned out over the water. A school of flying fish broke the surface, their silver bodies glinting in the sunlight as they skipped across the waves. He watched them in wonder, marveling at the simple beauty of nature.

For the first time in months, maybe even years, he felt truly at peace. The weight of his responsibilities, his guilt, his troubled relationships – all of it seemed to fade away, carried off by the gentle sea breeze. Here, on the open water with nothing but the horizon in sight, he was free.

He returned to the cabin and brewed a pot of coffee, savoring the rich aroma that filled the small space. He poured himself a mug and

THREE

returned to the deck, settling into a chair with his journal in hand. The pages lay open before him, but for once, he felt no urgency to write. Instead, he simply sat, sipping his coffee and watching the world come alive around him.

A pod of dolphins appeared off the starboard side, their sleek bodies arcing gracefully through the water. He set his mug down and moved to the railing, grinning as he watched their playful antics. One of the dolphins leapt high into the air, spinning before splashing back down. He laughed out loud, the sound carrying across the water.

As the sun climbed higher in the sky, he felt a renewed sense of energy coursing through him. He returned to the cabin and changed into his swim trunks, then climbed down the ladder at the stern of the boat. The water was cool and refreshing as he slipped beneath the surface.

He swam lazy laps around the boat, relishing the feel of the water against his skin. He floated on his back, staring up at the cloudless sky above. The worries that had plagued him on land seemed distant and insignificant now.

After his swim, he towelled off and prepared a simple breakfast of fruit and toast. He ate on the deck, watching as a pair of seagulls swooped and dove nearby.

He picked up his fishing rod, running his fingers along the familiar grooves of the handle. He baited the hook and cast his line, the rhythmic motion soothing and meditative. As he waited for a bite, he let his mind wander, not to the troubles of his past, but to the simple joys of the present.

The sun climbed higher, warming his skin and drying the last remnants of seawater from his hair. He closed his eyes, tilting his face up to the sky and basking in the warmth. For the first time in longer than he could remember, he felt truly alive.

* * *

Pete stood at the stern of the Harbinger, his fishing rod gripped firmly in his hands. The salty breeze whipping across his face brought a sense of calm he hadn't felt in months. He cast his line again, watching it arc through the air before disappearing beneath the surface with a soft plop.

Minutes ticked by, each one stretching into eternity as he waited for a bite. His thoughts drifted back to easier times when fishing was just a hobby, not an escape. He remembered weekends spent with his grandfather on his small motorboat, learning the intricacies of bait and tackle. Those memories were bittersweet now.

A sharp tug on the line snapped him back to the present. His heart raced as he felt the unmistakable weight of a fish on the other end. He reeled slowly, careful not to lose his catch. The rod bent under the strain, and he planted his feet wider on the deck for better balance.

"Come on, you bastard," he muttered through gritted teeth.

The fish fought hard, darting left and right in desperate attempts to shake the hook. His arms burned with the effort of keeping it steady, but he refused to give up. This catch represented more than just a meal; it was validation, proof that he could still succeed at something.

After what felt like an eternity of give and take, he saw a flash of silver beneath the waves. He leaned over the side, careful not to topple overboard, and reached for his net. With one final heave, he pulled the fish from the water and swung it onto the deck.

It was a mahi-mahi, its scales shimmering in vibrant hues of green and gold. Pete let out a triumphant whoop that echoed across the empty sea. He knelt beside his catch, admiring its size and beauty. It had to be at least thirty pounds, a respectable haul for any fisherman.

As he unhooked the fish, he felt a surge of pride. This was why he'd

THREE

come out here – to reconnect with that feeling of accomplishment, to prove to himself that he still had worth. He ran his hand along the mahi-mahi's smooth flank, marveling at the way its colors shifted in the sunlight.

He retrieved his phone from the cabin and snapped a few photos of his prize catch. He thought about sending them to Jennifer, sharing this moment of success with her, but hesitated. Their last conversation had been tense, filled with unspoken accusations and barely concealed resentment. Would she even care about his triumph out here on the open water?

Instead, he opened his messaging app and scrolled to Amy's name. His thumb hovered over the screen for a moment before he shook his head and put the phone away.

He carried the mahi-mahi to his small prep station, his movements practiced and efficient. He filleted the fish with care, setting aside the choicest cuts for dinner. The rest he wrapped and stored in the cooler, planning to smoke it later.

As the day wore on, his initial elation faded into a quieter contentment. He sat on the deck, legs dangling over the side, and watched the sun begin its descent toward the horizon.

He thought about his life back on land – the pressures of his practice, the strain in his marriage, the guilt of his affair. Out here, those problems seemed distant, almost insignificant. He wondered if he could stay out at sea forever, leaving behind the mess he'd made of his life.

But even as the thought crossed his mind, he knew it was impossible. Eventually, he'd have to return to face the consequences of his actions. For now, though, he could pretend that catching this fish was all that mattered in the world.

As evening approached, he fired up the small grill he'd brought along. The smell of grilling mahi-mahi filled the air, making his mouth water.

He seasoned the fish simply with salt, pepper, and a squeeze of lemon, wanting to savor its natural flavor.

He savored each bite of his hard-earned meal, washing it down with cold beer from his cooler. As he ate, he pulled out his journal and documented the day's success in detail. He described the fight with the fish, the pride he felt in landing it, and the simple pleasure of enjoying a meal he'd caught himself.

When he finished eating, he cleared away the dishes and returned to the deck. The sky had transformed into a brilliant canvas of oranges and pinks as the sun dipped below the horizon. He leaned against the railing, beer in hand, and let out a contented sigh.

As darkness fell and stars began to twinkle overhead, he made his way to the cabin. He fell asleep easily that night, lulled by the gentle rocking of the boat and the memory of his successful catch.

Pete's eyelids fluttered as he drifted into a deep slumber, the motion of the Harbinger lulling him into a dream state. The salty air faded away, replaced by the sweet scent of jasmine and vanilla.

He found himself standing in the kitchen of their cozy Frederiksted home. Sunlight streamed through the windows, casting a warm glow on the worn wooden floors. The sound of laughter drifted in from the backyard.

Jennifer stood at the counter, her auburn hair pulled back in a messy bun. She wore that faded blue apron he'd given her years ago, flour dusting her cheeks. Her hazel eyes sparkled as she looked up at him, a mischievous grin playing on her lips.

"You gonna help me with these pies, or just stand there lookin' pretty?" she said, holding out a rolling pin.

Pete chuckled, crossing the kitchen in a few strides. He took the rolling pin, his fingers brushing against hers.

"I thought that was my line," he said, earning an eye roll from Jennifer.

THREE

They worked side by side, rolling out dough and peeling apples. Pete snuck glances at his wife, marveling at the way her nose scrunched up when she concentrated. He'd forgotten how much he loved that little quirk.

"Remember our first attempt at baking together?" Jennifer said, breaking the comfortable silence.

Pete groaned, running a flour-covered hand through his hair.

"How could I forget? We nearly burned down the apartment."

Jennifer laughed, the sound light and carefree.

"And you insisted on eating that charred mess anyway."

"Hey, I slaved over that... whatever it was supposed to be," Pete said, playfully bumping her hip with his own.

She bumped him back, harder than he expected, sending a cloud of flour into the air. He blinked, momentarily stunned, before a wicked grin spread across his face.

"Oh, it's on," he said, scooping up a handful of flour.

Jennifer's eyes widened.

"Pete, don't you dare-"

But it was too late. He flung the flour, coating her in a fine white powder. She sputtered, wiping her face, before lunging for the flour bag.

What followed was nothing short of chaos. Flour flew through the air, coating every surface in the kitchen. Their laughter echoed off the walls as they ducked and dodged, pelting each other with handfuls of the powdery substance.

He caught Jennifer around the waist, both of them breathless and covered head to toe in flour. Her eyes met his, filled with joy and something deeper, something that made his heart ache with longing.

He leaned in, his lips just inches from hers. The world around them seemed to fade away, leaving only this moment, this connection between them.

"I love you," he whispered, the words carrying the weight of every unsaid emotion.

Jennifer's smile softened, her hand coming up to cup his cheek.

"I love you too, Pete. Always."

As their lips met, he felt a surge of warmth, of rightness. This was where he belonged, with Jennifer, in their little corner of the world.

The kiss deepened, and he pulled her closer, desperate to hold onto this feeling, this moment of perfect happiness.

But even as he clung to her, he felt the dream slipping away. The solid warmth of Jennifer in his arms faded, replaced by the cool morning air on the Harbinger.

Pete's eyes snapped open, his heart racing. For a moment, he couldn't remember where he was. The familiar walls of their kitchen were gone, replaced by the cramped confines of the boat's cabin.

He sat up, running a hand over his face. The dream clung to him, vivid and bittersweet. He could almost smell the flour in the air, feel the ghost of Jennifer's lips on his.

Reality crashed back in, leaving him feeling hollow. The happiness of the dream gave way to a gnawing guilt that twisted in his gut. He thought of Amy, of the secrets he kept from Jennifer, and shame washed over him.

He sat there for a long moment, head in his hands, trying to reconcile the man from his dream with the one he'd become.

He stood, making his way to the small porthole. Outside, the sun was just beginning to peek over the horizon.

He pressed his forehead against the cool glass, closing his eyes. The dream had stirred up feelings he'd been trying to bury, reminding him of the love he and Jennifer once shared. But it also highlighted how far he'd strayed from that path.

His chest tightened as he thought of Jennifer back home, unaware of his betrayal. He wondered if she ever dreamed of happier times, if she

THREE

missed the man he used to be.

Opening his eyes, he stared out at the endless sea before him. He'd come out here seeking escape, but he was beginning to realize that the thing he truly needed to escape from was himself.

With a heavy sigh, he turned away from the window. He reached for his journal, feeling a sudden need to write down the dream, to capture that fleeting moment of happiness before it slipped away entirely.

As he put pen to paper, he grappled with the conflicting emotions swirling within him. The love he still felt for Jennifer, the guilt over his affair with Amy, the longing for a simpler time - it all poured out onto the pages.

As Pete wrote, another memory surfaced. This time, it was Amy's face that filled his thoughts, her green eyes sparkling with mischief and affection.

It had been a lazy Sunday afternoon, just a few weeks ago. He had managed to sneak away from his responsibilities, citing a need to catch up on paperwork at the office. Instead, he'd found himself at Amy's cozy apartment, sprawled on her worn leather couch.

Amy was curled up next to him, her head resting on his chest. The scent of her shampoo, a mix of coconut and something floral, filled his nostrils. Outside, a sudden rainstorm erupted, drumming against the windows and creating a cocoon of intimacy around them.

"Tell me a secret," Amy whispered, her fingers tracing lazy patterns on his arm.

He chuckled, the sound rumbling in his chest.

"A secret? What kind of secret?"

She'd propped herself up on an elbow, her long blonde hair falling in a curtain around her face.

"Something you've never told anyone else. Something that's just for me."

He paused, considering. There were so many secrets he kept locked away, but in that moment, with Amy looking at him like he was the only person in the world, he felt a sudden urge to bare his soul.

"When I was a kid," he'd said, his voice low, "I used to pretend I was adopted. That my real parents were out there somewhere, looking for me."

Amy's eyebrows had knitted together in concern.

"Because of your dad?"

He nodded, surprised at how easily she'd understood.

"Yeah. I used to imagine this whole other life where my real father was… I don't know, kinder. More understanding."

Amy was quiet for a moment, her hand coming up to cup his cheek. "Oh, Pete," she murmured, her voice thick with emotion.

Then she leaned in and kissed him, soft and sweet, a gesture of comfort and acceptance that made his heart ache.

The memory dissolved. The contrast between his feelings for Jennifer and Amy was stark and unsettling. With Jennifer, there was history, commitment, a shared life built over years. But there was also tension, unspoken resentments, and a growing distance he couldn't seem to bridge.

Amy, on the other hand, represented something else entirely. She was spontaneity, passion, and a kind of uncomplicated affection that he'd been craving. With her, he felt seen and understood in a way he hadn't in years.

He climbed out of the cabin, needing fresh air to clear his head. The sun was high in the sky, beating down on the deck of the Harbinger. He squinted against the glare, taking in his surroundings.

The sea stretched out in all directions. The water was calm, with only gentle swells rocking the boat. He sighed. He could see a smudge of darkness in the distance. Dark clouds were gathering, a contrast to the clear blue sky overhead. He frowned, studying the formation.

THREE

It didn't look like much, probably just a small squall that would blow over quickly.

He thought about changing course, steering away from the potential bad weather. But the clouds were far off, and the day was so perfect. He didn't want to cut his trip short over what was likely nothing.

"It's fine," he muttered to himself. "Nothing to worry about."

Instead of altering his course, he decided to focus on fishing. He set up his gear, the familiar routine of preparing his rod and bait helping to settle his turbulent thoughts. As he cast his line into the water, he pushed away thoughts of Jennifer and Amy, of complicated relationships and uncertain futures.

For now, there was just this moment – the sun on his face, the sway of the boat, and the anticipation of the next big catch. He settled into his chair, his eyes fixed on the bobber floating on the water's surface. The dark clouds on the horizon faded from his mind, dismissed as inconsequential in the face of the perfect day.

Four

Pete's calloused fingers fumbled with the radio dial, his brow creased in concentration. the Harbinger rocked beneath him. He'd been out on the water for days now, the initial exhilaration of freedom giving way to a gnawing sense of isolation.

"Frederiksted Harbor, this is the Harbinger. Do you copy?" His voice crackled through the speaker, met only by the hiss of static.

He waited, counting the seconds, before trying again.

"Frederiksted Harbor, come in. This is the Harbinger requesting a weather update."

Nothing.

He glanced out the cabin window at the horizon. The sky was a canvas of purples and grays, promising rough seas ahead. He needed that weather report.

He adjusted the frequency, his movements more urgent now.

"This is the Harbinger calling any vessels in the area. Does anyone copy?"

The static crackled, a faint voice breaking through. He leaned in, straining to hear.

"…mayday…vessel…sinking…"

His heart rate spiked.

"This is the Harbinger. I copy your distress call. What's your position?"

FOUR

The voice came again, clearer this time.
"…coordinates…37°14'N 74°…"
And then it was gone, swallowed by the static.
"Dammit." Pete said, frantically adjusting the dial. "Come in, vessel in distress. Repeat your coordinates."
He was met with silence.
He slumped back in his chair, the weight of what he'd heard settling over him like a shroud. Someone out there was in trouble, possibly sinking, and he was powerless to help.
His gaze drifted to the flask of tequila on the counter. With the phantom voice of a sinking ship echoing in his ears, he was tempted.
He shook his head, forcing himself to focus. There had to be someone else out there, someone who could help. He changed frequencies again, this time reaching for the emergency channel.
"This is the Harbinger, broadcasting on emergency frequency. I've picked up a distress call from a vessel in trouble. Coordinates partially received as 37°14'N 74°. Any vessels in the area, please respond."
He repeated the message, his voice growing hoarse. Minutes ticked by, each one stretching into an eternity of silence. The freedom from people he'd sought now mocked him, a double-edged sword that cut deep.
Outside, the wind picked up, whistling through the rigging. the Harbinger's rocking became more pronounced, a foretaste of the storm to come. He glanced at his charts, trying to pinpoint his own position. He was far from any major shipping lanes, the realization settling like a stone in his gut.
He turned back to the radio, determination etched on his face.
"Frederiksted Harbor, this is the Harbinger. I repeat, this is the Harbinger. We have a potential emergency situation. Please respond."
The static hissed and popped, teasing him with half-formed sounds that might have been voices. He leaned closer, willing the radio to life

with every fiber of his being.

A burst of clarity cut through the white noise.

"…repeat…position…"

Pete's heart leaped.

"Yes! This is the Harbinger. I'm approximately 200 nautical miles southeast of St. Croix. I've picked up a distress call from a vessel at coordinates 37°14'N 74°…"

The voice faded, swallowed once more by the relentless static. He slammed his fist on the console. He was so close, yet so impossibly far from help or human contact.

The isolation pressed in on him, as tangible as the walls of the cabin. His eyes darted around, taking in the familiar contours of his boat. the Harbinger had always been his sanctuary, a floating piece of solitude where he could escape the complexities of life on land. Now, it felt more like a prison.

He thought of Jennifer, her practical voice a lifeline he desperately needed. Even Amy's impulsive energy would be welcome now, anything to break the silence. But there was only the wind, the waves, and the mocking hiss of the radio.

His gaze fell once more on the flask of tequila. Its presence nagged at him, a mystery he couldn't solve. He didn't remember packing it, yet here it was, offering a temporary escape from the crushing weight of his isolation.

With a shaking hand, he reached for the flask. The cool metal was a shock against his skin, grounding him in the moment. He unscrewed the cap, the sharp scent of alcohol cutting through the salty air.

Just as he was about to take a swig, the radio crackled to life. "…Harbinger…repeat…storm warning…"

Pete froze, the flask halfway to his lips. He set it down with a thunk, lunging for the radio.

"Yes! This is the Harbinger. I copy. Please repeat storm warning."

FOUR

But the voice was gone, leaving Pete with more questions than answers. The wind outside howled louder, as if to underscore the unseen danger lurking on the horizon. His isolation felt more acute than ever, a yawning chasm between him and the rest of the world.

He stared at the silent radio, willing it to speak again. But there was only static, a ceaseless reminder of how alone he truly was.

The sea churned, its once placid surface now a roiling mass of gray-green swells. He white-knuckled the wheel of the Harbinger. The boat pitched and rolled, mirroring the turbulence in his mind.

He squinted at the horizon, searching for a break in the clouds. There was none. The sky had darkened to a foreboding slate. Spray from the waves lashed his face, stinging his eyes and leaving a salty residue on his lips.

His stomach clenched, a familiar sensation of dread creeping up his spine. It wasn't just the weather that unsettled him. The choppy waters stirred up memories he'd long tried to suppress.

The wheel jerked in his hands, and he was no longer on the Harbinger. He was eighteen again, standing in his father's study, the air thick with tension and unspoken disappointment.

Jonathon Corbin sat behind his desk, a weathered atlas spread open before him. His steel-blue eyes bored into Pete, making him feel small and insignificant.

"Psychiatry?" Jonathon's voice dripped with disdain. "You want to waste your life listening to other people's problems?"

Pete squared his shoulders, fighting the urge to shrink away.

"It's not a waste, Dad. I can help people."

Jonathon snorted, the sound harsh and dismissive.

"Help people? What about helping yourself? What about the family business?"

Pete's hands clenched at his sides. The Corbin Shipping Company had been his father's pride and joy for decades. It was also a noose around Pete's neck, a future he'd never wanted but felt powerless to escape.

"I'm not cut out for that life," Pete said.

Jonathon's face darkened. He stood, his imposing frame casting a shadow across the room.

"Not cut out for it? You're a Corbin. It's in your blood."

Pete took a step back, bumping into a bookshelf. A framed photo of his father standing proudly on the deck of a cargo ship teetered precariously.

"I want to make my own path," Pete said, finding a reserve of courage he didn't know he possessed. "I want to understand people, to make a difference in their lives."

Jonathon's laugh was cold and humorless.

"Understand people? You can barely understand yourself, boy. You think you can fix others when you're such a mess?"

Pete flinched, feeling the sting of truth in his father's cruel assessment.

"I'm not a mess," Pete said weakly, but the words rang hollow even to his own ears.

Jonathon moved around the desk, closing the distance between them. His presence was suffocating, filling the room with disapproval and barely contained anger.

"You're throwing away everything I've built," Jonathon growled. "Everything I've worked for. And for what? To sit in an office and listen to rich people whine about their problems?"

Pete's resolve wavered. He could feel his dreams slipping away, crushed under the weight of his father's expectations.

"It's more than that," he mumbled.

Jonathon jabbed a finger into Pete's chest.

"You're weak, Pete. Always have been. I thought you'd grow out of it, but here you are, running away from real responsibility."

FOUR

Pete's vision blurred, tears threatening to spill over. He blinked them back furiously, refusing to give his father the satisfaction of seeing him cry.

"I'm not running away," Pete said, his voice cracking. "I'm choosing my own path."

Jonathon's face contorted with disgust.

"Your own path? You're lost, boy. You always have been. And now you want to drag others down with you."

The words echoed in Pete's mind, a cruel mantra that had haunted him for years. Lost. Weak. A disappointment.

"I'm not lost," Pete whispered, but he wasn't sure who he was trying to convince anymore.

Jonathon turned away, his broad shoulders rigid with anger.

"Get out of my sight," he said. "Go play doctor if that's what you want. But don't come crawling back when you realize what a mistake you've made."

Pete stumbled out of the study, his father's words ringing in his ears. The hallway seemed to go on forever, the portraits of Corbin ancestors lining the walls watching him with judging eyes.

He burst out of the house, gulping in the air. The world spun around him, his father's study fading away like a bad dream.

Pete found himself back on the Harbinger, his hands clenched so tightly on the wheel that his fingers ached. The sea raged around him, waves crashing against the hull with increasing ferocity.

He blinked, trying to shake off the lingering echoes of his father's voice. The memory had left him shaken, reopening old wounds he thought had long since healed.

The boat lurched violently, nearly throwing him off his feet. He steadied himself, forcing his attention back to the present. The storm was worsening, the sky now an ominous black blanket streaked with lightning.

His heart-rate quickened, adrenaline coursing through his veins. He needed to focus, to navigate through this tempest. But his father's words kept repeating in his mind, a cruel soundtrack to the chaos around him.

Lost. Weak. A disappointment.

The wind howled, drowning out his thoughts. He gritted his teeth, fighting against the wheel as the Harbinger was buffeted by another massive wave. He was not that scared eighteen-year-old boy anymore. He had made something of himself, hadn't he?

But as the storm raged on, he couldn't shake the feeling that maybe, just maybe, his father had been right all along. Maybe he was lost, adrift in more ways than one.

The choppy waves slapped against the hull, rocking the boat with increasing force. Pete's stomach churned with a mix of anxiety and seasickness.

A flash of movement caught his eye. He squinted, scanning the sky above. At first, he saw nothing but the roiling clouds. Then, a dark shape emerged from the gloom.

An albatross.

It was massive, larger than any seabird he had ever seen. Its wingspan stretched impossibly wide, dwarfing the gulls that scattered in its wake. The bird wheeled overhead, tracing lazy circles above the Harbinger.

Pete's breath caught in his throat. He'd heard the old sailors' tales, whispered over beers at the marina. Albatrosses were bad luck, harbingers of doom for those foolish enough to sail beneath them.

"Get a grip, Corbin," he muttered. "It's just a godamm bird."

But as the albatross continued its relentless circling, Pete found it harder to dismiss the growing sense of foreboding that settled in his gut. The bird's beady eyes seemed to fix on him, following his every move.

FOUR

Pete turned away, focusing on the controls. He needed to prepare for the coming storm, not waste time worrying about some superstitious bullshit. He adjusted the sails, battening down the hatches as the wind howled around him.

Still, he couldn't shake the feeling of being watched.

When he glanced up again, the albatross had drawn closer. It glided just above the mast, its enormous wings casting a shadow over the deck. Pete could make out every detail now – the hooked beak, the mottled feathers, the talons that looked sharp enough to shred flesh.

A chill ran down his spine. This was no ordinary bird. There was something unnatural about it, something almost... demonic.

The albatross let out a harsh cry that cut through the wind. It sounded like a laugh, mocking and cruel. Pete flinched, nearly losing his grip on the wheel.

"Go away!" he shouted, his voice cracking. "Leave me alone!"

But the bird paid no heed to his cries. Pete could have sworn he saw a glint of intelligence in its eyes, a malevolent awareness that went beyond animal instinct.

He remembered the stories his grandfather used to tell, tales of sailors driven mad by loneliness and guilt. Of phantom birds that haunted men at sea, tormenting them until they leaped into the waves to escape.

His hands were shaking as he reached for the radio. He needed to hear a human voice, to anchor himself to reality. But when he flipped the switch, all he heard was static.

The albatross screamed again, the sound cutting through the white noise like a knife. Pete dropped the radio, stumbling back against the cabin door.

"This isn't real," he whispered, squeezing his eyes shut. "It's not real. It's not real."

His mind struggled, grasping for an explanation. Was this some sort of hallucination? A product of stress and isolation? Ever the psychiatrist.

The wind howled louder, drowning out his thoughts. Rain began to fall, fat drops splattering against the deck. The storm was upon him, but he couldn't tear his eyes away from the albatross.

It spread its wings, the span seeming to stretch impossibly wide. For a moment, it blotted out the sky entirely, leaving Pete in a world of shadow and feathers.

Then, with a final piercing cry, it elevated. Pete watched as it soared away, disappearing into the gathering storm clouds.

He sagged against the wheel, his heart pounding. The encounter had left him shaken to his core.

As the first lightning bolt split the sky, he steadied himself for what was to come. He had a feeling that the storm – both outside and within his mind – was only just beginning.

Five

The sky darkened with alarming speed, transforming the once tranquil sea into a churning cauldron of fury. Pete's stomach lurched as the Harbinger pitched violently, tossed about like a toy in a child's bathtub. He fought to keep the boat steady against the onslaught of wind and waves.

Rain lashed against his face, stinging his eyes and blurring his vision. The air filled with the roar of thunder, punctuated by flashes of lightning that illuminated the tempest in stark, terrifying clarity. His heart was pounding against his ribcage as if trying to escape the chaos surrounding him.

He scanned the skies, searching for any sign of the albatross that had been his stalker before. The bird had vanished, swallowed by the storm or fled to safer skies.

A massive wave crashed over the bow, drenching Pete and flooding the deck. He sputtered and coughed, spitting out seawater that tasted of salt and fear. The boat groaned under the assault, timbers creaking in protest as the sea tried to tear it apart.

Pete stumbled across the slick deck, fighting his way to the radio. He had to try again to call for help, to let someone know he was out here, lost in this nightmare of wind and water. His fingers, numb with cold, fumbled with the dials.

"Mayday, mayday," he shouted into the microphone, his voice

cracking. "This is the Harbinger. I'm caught in a storm, coordinates unknown. Please, if anyone can hear me—"

Static answered him, crackling and hissing like the angry sea itself. He slammed his fist against the useless device, frustration and terror warring within him. He was alone out here, truly alone, with no one to hear his cries for help.

Another wave smashed into the boat, sending him sprawling across the cabin floor. He crashed into the galley table, pain exploding in his side as his ribs connected with the unforgiving wood. Gasping, he pulled himself up, knowing that to stay down was to invite disaster.

The boat lurched again, and he heard a sickening crack from somewhere below. Water began to seep in through the floorboards, a thin trickle at first, then a steady stream. Panic clawed at his throat as he realized the Harbinger was taking on water.

He scrambled for the bilge pump, praying it would be enough to keep them afloat. The machine sputtered to life, but he could see it was a losing battle. For every gallon pumped out, two more seemed to rush in.

Lightning split the sky, followed immediately by a thunderclap so loud it could be physically felt. His ears rang, disorienting him further. He stumbled back to the wheel, fighting to keep the Harbinger pointed into the waves. To turn broadside now would mean certain capsizing.

The rain intensified, sheets of water falling from the sky with such force that he could barely breathe. It was as if the entire ocean had turned against him, determined to drag him down into its depths.

Hours seemed to pass, though he had lost all sense of time. His arms ached from the constant struggle with the wheel, his body battered and bruised from being thrown about the cabin. Exhaustion pulled at him, tempting him to give in, to let go and let the sea take him.

But something in him refused to surrender. He thought of all the patients who depended on him, of the lives he'd helped put back together. He thought of the unresolved conflicts with his loved ones, the words left unsaid. He couldn't let this be the end, not like this.

With determination, he fought on. He battled each wave, each gust of wind, pouring every ounce of strength he had into keeping the Harbinger afloat and on course. The storm raged around him, unrelenting in its fury, but he matched it with a fierce will to survive.

* * *

The boat pitched and rolled beneath Pete's feet as he struggled to maintain his balance.

He stumbled toward the cabin door. He gripped the frame, knuckles white, and surveyed the chaos unfolding around him. Loose items skittered across the deck with each violent lurch of the vessel. His fishing gear, once neatly stowed, now threatened to become deadly projectiles.

"Dammit," he said, his words lost in the roar of the wind.

He took a couple of deep breaths, preparing himself for the task ahead. With one hand firmly grasping the railing, he inched his way along the deck. The boat heaved beneath him, and he nearly lost his footing. Salt water stung his eyes as another wave broke over the bow.

He reached the first of the loose items – a tackle box that had come unlatched in the commotion. He snatched it up, hugging it to his chest as he made his way back to the cabin. Inside, he shoved it into a storage compartment, wedging it tight to prevent further movement.

Back on deck, he spotted his favorite fishing rod sliding dangerously close to the edge. He lunged for it, his fingers closing around the handle just as a particularly violent wave struck the boat. The force of the impact sent him sprawling, and for a heart-stopping moment, he thought he might go overboard.

He clung to the rod and the nearest railing, his body pressed flat against the deck. The sea seemed determined to claim him, to drag him into its depths. He could almost hear it calling his name, a siren song barely heard beneath the howling wind.

"Not today," he growled, pushing himself to his feet.

He secured the fishing rod in its holder and turned his attention to the rest of the deck. A cooler had overturned, spilling its contents across the wet surface. He said, "Shit," under his breath as he saw several of his prized lures mixed in with the ice and bait.

Bending down, he began to gather the scattered items. His fingers, numb from the cold and wet, fumbled with each piece. A particularly garish lure – one his grandfather had given him years ago – slipped from his grasp and skittered across the deck.

He lunged for it, his body stretching out as his fingertips brushed the lure's edge. Just then, the boat lurched violently to starboard. The sudden movement sent him sliding across the wet deck, his body slamming into the railing with bruising force.

For a moment, he lay there, stunned and gasping for breath. The pain in his side was sharp, but the adrenaline coursing through his veins dulled it to a manageable throb. He pushed himself up, scanning the deck for the lost lure. It was gone, claimed by the sea like so much else in his life.

The loss of the lure struck him harder than he expected. It wasn't just a piece of fishing equipment; it was a tangible link to his past. Now it was gone, swallowed by the same unforgiving waters that threatened to consume him.

Shaking off the momentary melancholy, he refocused on the task at hand. He gathered the remaining items from the cooler, shoving them haphazardly back inside. With a grunt of effort, he dragged the cooler across the deck and secured it with a length of rope he found nearby.

FIVE

The wind seemed to intensify, if that was even possible. It shrieked through the rigging, a banshee wail that sent shivers down his spine. He squinted against the stinging spray, searching for any other items that needed securing.

A flash of movement caught his eye. His heart sank as he realized his journal had come loose from its usual spot. The wind had caught its pages, threatening to tear them out and scatter his thoughts across the angry sea.

He scrambled toward the book, his feet slipping on the wet deck. He dove, arms outstretched, and managed to snag the journal just as a particularly strong gust tried to lift it away. Clutching it to his chest, he rolled onto his back, panting from the exertion.

For a moment, he lay there, the journal pressed against him like a shield. In it were his most private thoughts, his fears, his hopes – the unvarnished truth of who he was. The idea of losing it to the storm filled him with a dread that rivaled his fear of the raging sea itself.

He opened the book, checking for any missing pages. To his relief, it seemed intact. He closed it carefully, then tucked it securely into his jacket, zipping it tight against his chest. At least now, if the worst should happen, his words would go down with him.

The sea's dark waves rose like mountains against the stormy sky.

A monstrous wave towered before the boat, dwarfing all that had come before. Pete's heart hammered in his chest as he realized the true scale of the behemoth bearing down on him. It was a wall of water, impossibly high and terrifyingly close.

The wave struck with the force of a freight train. the Harbinger pitched violently, tilting at a sickening angle. His feet left the deck as the boat tipped precariously to port. His stomach dropped, a sensation of freefall gripping him as the world tilted on its axis.

Water crashed over the railings, flooding the deck. The salt spray filled his mouth. He coughed and sputtered, struggling to breathe as the deluge threatened to sweep him overboard.

For a heart-stopping moment, he thought the boat would capsize. the Harbinger groaned under the strain, her hull creaking in protest. His body slammed against the cabin wall, the impact knocking the wind from his lungs.

"Come on, baby," he pleaded, his voice raw. "Don't give up on me now."

The boat teetered on the edge of disaster, balancing on a knife's edge between righting itself and succumbing to the sea's wrath.

With a final, gut-wrenching thrust, the Harbinger began to right herself. Pete's feet found traction on the slick deck once more. He stumbled, barely managing to keep his footing as the boat leveled out.

Gasping for air, he surveyed the damage. Water sloshed across the deck, carrying loose items in its wake. A fishing rod clattered against the railing before disappearing over the side. The main sail hung in tatters, shredded by the gale-force winds.

Pete's legs trembled, the adrenaline leaving him weak and shaky.

"That was too close," he muttered.

As if in response, a flash of lightning illuminated the sky, followed by a deafening crack of thunder. Pete flinched, his nerves frayed to the breaking point.

The storm showed no signs of abating. If anything, it seemed to be intensifying. The waves continued to batter the Harbinger, each impact sending shudders through the boat's frame.

Another wave crashed over the bow, sending a fresh torrent of water across the deck.

A flash of movement caught Pete's eye. Something large and dark overhead, barely visible against the storm-darkened sky. He squinted, trying to make out the shape through the driving rain.

For a moment, he thought he glimpsed the albatross, its massive

FIVE

wings spread wide as it circled the beleaguered boat. But that was impossible. No bird could fly in this maelstrom.

He rubbed his eyes, trying to clear his vision. When he looked again, there was nothing but roiling clouds and sheets of rain. He must have imagined it, a trick of the light or a product of his fear-addled mind.

Pushing the unsettling image aside, he focused on the task at hand. He had to get below deck, check the pumps, and pray that the Harbinger's hull remained intact. It was going to be a long, terrifying night, and he wasn't sure if he—or his boat—would make it through to see the dawn.

* * *

Pete realized the navigation console, once securely bolted to the deck, had vanished. He stumbled over to where it had been. Nothing remained but a few frayed wires and bent bolts.

"No, no, no," he said, panic rising in his throat. He scanned the roiling sea, hoping against hope to catch a glimpse of the equipment. But there was nothing but endless gray waves and stinging rain.

Without the GPS and radar, he was blind. The storm had already thrown him far off course, and now he had no way to find his way back. He was lost, adrift in the vastness of the Caribbean.

He needed to think, to come up with a plan, but the relentless assault of the storm made it impossible to focus.

He staggered back to the wheel, gripping it tightly to steady himself. As he did, his foot struck something solid that skittered across the deck. He frowned, reaching down to retrieve the object. His fingers closed around cool metal, and he lifted it up for inspection.

It was a sextant, its brass body tarnished with age but still intact. He stared at it in disbelief, turning it over in his hands. He'd never owned a sextant, let alone brought one on board the Harbinger. Yet here it was, as if conjured from thin air.

The instrument was beautiful in its complexity, a relic from a bygone era of seafaring. Intricate gears and dials adorned its surface, and the lens caught what little light remained, glinting dully. He ran his thumb over an engraving on the base: "N.C. 1876."

"Where the hell did you come from?" he muttered.

He wracked his brain, trying to remember if he'd seen the sextant before. Had it been tucked away in some forgotten corner of the boat? But no, he knew every inch of the Harbinger. He'd have noticed something like this.

A chill ran through him that had nothing to do with the rain soaking him to the bone. First the mysterious flask of whiskey, now this. It was as if the boat was playing tricks on him, revealing secrets he didn't know it held.

He clutched the sextant tightly, unsure whether to be grateful for its appearance or unnerved by it. He'd learned the basics of celestial navigation years ago, a skill he'd never thought he'd need to use. Now, it might be his only chance of finding his way home.

But as he looked up at the sky, his heart sank. The storm had blotted out the stars, leaving nothing but an impenetrable blanket of clouds. Even if he knew how to use the antique instrument properly, it was useless without a clear view of the heavens.

Another wave crashed over the boat, nearly tearing the sextant from his grasp. He stumbled, clutching it tightly. In that moment, the absurdity of his situation hit him. Here he was, in the middle of a raging storm, holding onto an antique navigation tool that had appeared out of nowhere, while his state-of-the-art equipment lay at the bottom of the sea.

A hysterical laugh bubbled up in his throat, quickly swallowed by the

FIVE

howling wind. He was losing it, he realized. The isolation, the stress, the relentless battering of the storm – it was all taking its toll on his mind.

He made his way back to the wheel, the sextant still clutched in one hand. He had to focus, had to keep the Harbinger afloat until the storm passed. Only then could he worry about where he was and how to get back.

As he gripped the wheel, his eyes were drawn to the sextant once more. In the dim light of the storm, he could have sworn he saw something moving within the intricate gears. A play of shadows, perhaps, or a trick of his exhausted mind. But for a moment, it seemed as if the ancient instrument was alive, ticking away the seconds of some cosmic clock.

He couldn't afford to let his imagination run wild, not now. But as he turned his attention back to the churning sea before him, he couldn't shake the feeling that the sextant was more than just an unexpected tool. It felt like a message, a sign – though of what, he couldn't begin to guess.

The storm raged on, and he clung to the wheel of the Harbinger, a man caught between the modern world he'd left behind and the ancient mysteries of the sea. The sextant weighed heavy in his hand, a tangible reminder that on this journey, nothing was as it seemed.

Six

The storm's fury ebbed, leaving Pete slumped against the helm. His muscles ached, and his breath was labored. He blinked, trying to clear the salt spray from his eyes. The world around him seemed to spin and tilt, as if the sea's chaos had seeped into his very bones.

He stumbled to his feet, his legs wobbly beneath him. He gripped the railing, steadying himself as he surveyed the damage. The deck was a mess of tangled lines and scattered gear. A fishing rod lay snapped in two near the stern, and the tackle box had spilled its contents across the deck.

He shuffled forward, careful not to slip on the wet surface. The sky above was a patchwork of breaking clouds, hints of blue peeking through. The sea, moments ago a roiling monster, now lapped gently against the hull.

His mind felt foggy, his thoughts as jumbled as the debris on the deck. He tried to recall how long the storm had lasted, but time had become a fluid, unreliable thing. Hours? Days? It could have been an eternity for all he knew.

He made his way to the cabin, ducking inside to escape the lingering drizzle. The interior was a mirror of the deck's chaos. Books lay strewn across the floor, and a shattered mug left a trail of cold coffee across the galley counter.

SIX

He flipped open his journal, intending to record the storm's passing, but found himself staring at a blank page. The words wouldn't come. How could he describe what he'd just experienced? The terror, the helplessness, the certainty that each moment might be his last?

He closed the journal and set it aside. He needed to get his bearings, to figure out where the storm had taken him. He moved to the navigation station, only to remember the equipment had been swept overboard. The antique sextant sat in its place, a brass relic that seemed to mock his modern helplessness.

He picked it up, its weight unfamiliar in his hands. He had basic knowledge of celestial navigation, a skill his father had insisted he learn, but he'd never had to use it. Now, staring at the intricate device, he felt a pang of regret for not paying closer attention to those lessons.

He stepped back onto the deck, sextant in hand. The sky had cleared further. The sun was low on the horizon, but whether it was rising or setting, he couldn't tell. His internal clock was as scrambled as his sense of direction.

He raised the sextant to his eye, attempting to take a reading. The instrument felt alien in his grip, and he struggled to hold it steady. After several frustrating attempts, he lowered it, no closer to determining his position than before.

He needed to assess the damage to the boat and see what supplies remained. the Harbinger had weathered the storm, but he couldn't be sure of her seaworthiness without a thorough inspection.

He began at the bow, working his way aft. The hull seemed intact, with no signs of major damage. The sails, however, were another story. The main had a long tear along its edge, and the jib was in tatters. Without them, he'd be relying solely on the engine to get home.

The rest of his inspection revealed minor damage – scrapes and dents in the hull, a broken porthole, missing cushions from the deck chairs. Nothing catastrophic, but the cumulative effect was unsettling. the

Harbinger felt different, changed somehow by the storm's violence.

He returned to the helm, his exhaustion catching up with him. He needed rest, but the thought of sleep filled him with dread. What if he woke to find himself in the midst of another storm? Or worse, what if he didn't wake at all?

He glanced at the horizon, searching for any sign of land or other vessels. Nothing but endless blue met his gaze. The isolation pressed in on him.

As the sun dipped lower, he felt the first stirrings of true fear. The storm had passed, but he was far from safe. Lost, disoriented, and ill-equipped, he faced a challenge unlike any he'd encountered in his comfortable life ashore.

He gripped the wheel. the Harbinger bobbed gently on the calm sea, waiting for his next move. But he found himself paralyzed, unsure of which direction to take. Every choice seemed dangerous, every option a potential path to disaster.

He scanned the horizon, searching for any familiar landmark, a hint of land, or another vessel. Still nothing in every direction.

His breath came in short, sharp gasps. The realization hit: he was lost. Completely and utterly lost.

The boat rocked gently on the calm sea, but his world spun. His heart hammered, threatening to burst from his chest. Sweat beaded on his forehead despite the cool breeze.

He stumbled to the cabin, searching for the radio. His fingers slipped on the dials as he tried to tune in to any frequency. Static crackled through the speakers, mocking his efforts.

"Mayday. Mayday. This is the Harbinger. I'm lost at sea. Can anyone hear me?"

Only white noise answered him.

He slumped against the wall, sliding to the floor. His chest con-

SIX

stricted, each breath a struggle. The cabin walls seemed to close in, the air growing thick and heavy.

He clawed at his shirt collar, desperate for air. Dark spots danced at the edges of his vision. Was this how it ended? Lost and alone, gasping for breath on the floor of his boat?

A memory flashed through his mind: his father's stern face, disappointment etched in every line.

"You're not cut out for this, Pete. The sea's no place for weaklings."

He squeezed his eyes shut, trying to block out the memory. But his father's words echoed in his head, mixing with the static from the radio.

He forced himself to his feet, staggering out onto the deck. The ocean stretched before him, endless and indifferent to his plight.

He tried to focus on his breathing, to slow the frantic beating of his heart. In. Out. In. Out.

But panic clawed at him, refusing to loosen its grip. What if he never found his way back? What if he drifted out here forever, until his supplies ran out and he wasted away to nothingness?

He thought of Jennifer, her practical voice a lifeline in his mind. What would she do in this situation? Stay calm, he imagined her saying. Think it through.

But calm felt impossible. His mind conjured images of slow starvation, of sharks circling his drifting vessel, of rescue ships passing by just over the horizon, never knowing he was there.

Hiss legs gave out, and he sank to the deck. He pressed his forehead against the cool metal of the railing, trying to ground himself in the physical sensation.

Slowly, gradually, the vice around his chest began to loosen. The roaring in his ears subsided.

As his panic ebbed, exhaustion took its place. He dragged himself back to the cabin, collapsing onto his bunk.

* * *

Pete's eyes snapped open, his heart racing. The rocking of the boat felt disorienting. He blinked, trying to shake off the fog of sleep that clung to him like a shroud. The cabin was dark, save for the faint glow of starlight filtering through the porthole.

He fumbled for his watch, squinting at the luminous dial. 2:15 AM. He'd only slept for a couple of hours, but it felt like days. His mouth was dry, his tongue sticking to the roof of his mouth like sandpaper.

He hauled himself up, muscles protesting. He stumbled to the galley, groping for a water bottle. The cool liquid hit his parched throat, and he gulped greedily. Some of it dribbled down his chin, soaking into his shirt.

The boat creaked and groaned around him, a symphony of unfamiliar noises that set his nerves on edge. He made his way to the deck, the cool night air hitting him like a slap to the face.

The sky stretched out above him, a blanket of blackness studded with countless pinpricks of light. Under different circumstances, it might have been beautiful. Now, it felt oppressive, overwhelming.

He fumbled in his pocket for the antique sextant he'd found earlier. The brass was cool against his skin, its weight oddly comforting. He held it up, trying to remember the lessons his father had drilled into him years ago.

"You never know when you might need this, boy," Jonathon's gruff voice echoed in his memory. "Electronics fail. The stars don't."

Pete's hands shook as he tried to align the sextant with the horizon. The stars blurred and swam before his eyes, refusing to cooperate. He blinked hard, willing his vision to clear.

"Come on," he muttered, frustration building. "Come on, damn it."

But the more he tried, the more confused he became. The constel-

SIX

lations that should have been familiar looked all wrong. Orion's belt seemed to twist and writhe, the stars rearranging themselves.

He lowered the sextant. Sweat beaded on his forehead despite the cool night air. He closed his eyes, counting to ten, trying to slow his racing heart.

When he opened them again, the sky looked normal. But the damage was done. Doubt had taken root, spreading through his mind like a cancer.

He stumbled back to the cabin, collapsing into a chair.

He buried his face in his hands, his shoulders shaking. He wasn't sure if he was laughing or crying. Maybe both. The line between the two seemed as blurred as the stars had been.

He returned to the deck, his legs threatening to give out beneath him.

He looked up at the stars again, searching for something, anything familiar. But they remained stubbornly alien, twinkling down at him with coldness.

He couldn't believe how lost he was. Not just on the ocean, but in the labyrinth of his own mind.

He gasped, struggling to breathe, to think, to do anything but panic again.

But panic was all he had left. It rose in him like a tide, threatening to sweep away the last vestiges of his sanity. He closed his eyes, willing it to stop, to go away, to leave him in peace.

But there was no peace to be found. Not out here, in the endless night. Not in the abyss of his own fractured psyche.

He slid down to the deck, his back against the railing. He hugged his knees to his chest, making himself as small as possible. As if by shrinking himself, he could somehow make the vast, uncaring universe around him less overwhelming.

He stayed there, shivering in the night air, until the first hints of dawn began to lighten the eastern sky. But even as the darkness receded, the shadows in his mind remained, deep and impenetrable.

* * *

Pete's eyes fluttered open, squinting against the harsh sunlight that streamed through the cabin windows. His head throbbed, a dull ache that pulsed behind his eyes. He blinked, trying to orient himself.

He pushed himself up, his muscles protesting with every movement. The cabin swayed before his eyes, and he gripped the edge of his bunk to steady himself. How long had he been out? When did he come back into the cabin?

He fumbled for his watch, but his wrist was bare. He frowned, scanning the small space for any sign of it. Nothing. The realization hit him like a punch to the gut - he had no idea what time it was, or even what day.

He stumbled to his feet, lurching towards the cabin door. The bright Caribbean sun assaulted his senses as he stepped onto the deck.

His beard seemed to have grown thicker, rougher against his palm. Had days passed?

The deck of the Harbinger was a mess. Empty food wrappers fluttered in the breeze, caught in the nooks and crannies of the boat. His stomach growled, a sharp reminder of his physical state.

He made his way to the galley, hoping to find some indication of the passage of time. The calendar he'd hung on the wall was gone, leaving behind only a faded rectangle where it once hung. He yanked open the refrigerator, recoiling at the smell. The perishables had long since spoiled, a testament to his extended unconsciousness.

He stumbled back onto the deck, his eyes scanning the horizon, once again, for any sign of land or other vessels. Nothing but water. The

SIX

sun beat down mercilessly, and He realized how parched he was. He needed water, and fast.

He made his way to the water tank, praying it hadn't been compromised during the storm. The gauge showed it was nearly empty, but there was enough for a few days if he rationed carefully. He cupped his hands under the spout, bringing the cool liquid to his cracked lips. It tasted like life itself.

His skin was weathered, his eyes sunken and haunted. The beard that had grown in was peppered with gray, making him look years older.

"What happened to me?" he whispered, his voice hoarse from disuse.

His eyes landed on his fishing rod, still secured in its holder. An idea struck him. If he could catch something, he might be able to determine how long he'd been adrift based on the size of his catch.

He grabbed the rod, his movements clumsy and uncoordinated. He baited the hook as his hands trembled, casting the line out into the calm waters. As he waited, his mind wandered to Jennifer.

The thought of never seeing her again, of dying alone out here on the ocean, threatened to overwhelm him. He closed his eyes. He needed to focus, to survive.

Hours passed with no bite. The sun began to dip towards the horizon, painting the sky in vibrant hues of orange and pink. He reeled in his line, defeated. He'd have to try again tomorrow.

Seven

The day had been long, filled with fruitless attempts at navigation and growing despair. As darkness settled over the sea, Pete felt a chill run through him.

A flicker of movement caught his eye. He squinted, peering into the twilight. There, high above the boat, a familiar silhouette emerged.

The albatross had returned.

Its wingspan stretched impossibly wide, blotting out patches of stars as it glided in lazy circles. He'd hoped the bird's earlier appearance was a fluke, a random encounter. Now, as it wheeled overhead with eerie persistence, he couldn't shake the feeling of being watched.

"Just a bird," he muttered, but the words rang hollow.

The albatross dipped lower. It seemed to study him, head cocked to one side as it rode the air currents. His skin crawled. He'd heard the old sailors' tales about albatrosses, how they carried the souls of dead mariners. How killing one brought a curse upon a ship.

"I haven't killed you," he said, his voice hoarse. "So why are you here?"

The bird offered no answer, continuing its silent vigil. As night deepened, Pete found himself unable to look away. The albatross's presence filled him with dread, as if it knew something he didn't. As if it was waiting for something to happen.

He shook his head, trying to clear the fog of superstition from his mind. He was a man of science, a psychiatrist. He dealt in facts, not

SEVEN

folklore. And yet...

He remembered his grandfather's gruff voice, telling him about signs and omens at sea. How nature spoke to those who knew how to listen. He had scoffed then, but now, lost in the vastness of the ocean, those old warnings didn't seem so foolish.

The albatross swooped even lower, and Pete ducked instinctively. Its massive wings stirred the air, sending a gust of wind across the deck. For a moment, he could have sworn he smelled something foul, like rotting fish and seaweed.

He stumbled back. This was no ordinary bird. It couldn't be. The way it moved, the unnatural size of it – everything about the albatross felt wrong.

He fumbled for his journal, needing to document this, to prove to himself he wasn't going mad. He scribbled down his observations, the words spilling across the page in a frantic scrawl.

The albatross is back. Bigger than before. It won't leave. Can't shake the feeling it's watching me. Waiting for something. What does it want?

Pete looked up from the journal, and his breath caught in his throat. The albatross hovered directly above the boat, its wings spread wide like some avenging angel. In the starlight, its feathers gleamed with an oily sheen that made Pete's stomach turn.

He blinked, and for a split second, he could have sworn the bird's form shifted. Instead of feathers, he saw scales. Instead of a beak, rows of razor-sharp teeth. But then he blinked again, and it was just a bird once more.

He stumbled below deck, slamming the hatch behind him. His chest heaved as he slumped against the wall, trying to make sense of what he'd seen.

What would Jenn say if she could see him now, cowering from a fucking bird? He could almost hear her voice, gently chiding him for letting his imagination run wild.

But Jennifer wasn't here. He was alone, lost at sea with only his thoughts and that damned albatross for company.

He closed his eyes, willing the bird to disappear. But even with his eyes shut, he could feel its presence. It was out there, circling, waiting. For what, he didn't know. But as the night wore on and sleep eluded him, one thing became clear: the albatross wasn't going anywhere.

He tossed and turned in his bunk. Every creak of the hull, every splash of water against the side, sent his heart racing. He imagined the albatross perched on the deck, its inhuman eyes peering through the walls at him.

When dawn finally broke, he emerged from below deck, bleary-eyed and on edge. He half-expected to find the boat covered in feathers or claw marks, some tangible proof of the albatross's vigil.

But the Harbinger looked the same as always. The only sign that anything was amiss was the lone figure wheeling in the sky above, its wings spread wide against the pink-tinged clouds.

He stared up at the albatross, a mix of fear and defiance coursing through him. Whatever game this bird was playing, whatever omen it represented, he refused to be cowed by it. He was Dr. Pete Corbin, respected psychiatrist and experienced sailor. He wouldn't let some oversized seagull get the better of him.

And yet, as the sun climbed higher and the albatross maintained its unwavering presence, he couldn't shake the feeling that something fundamental had shifted. The ocean had become an arena, and he was at the center of it, with the albatross as both spectator and judge.

* * *

SEVEN

Pete stared at the horizon, his eyes unfocused and bloodshot from lack of sleep. It was nearing dusk.

A gust of wind ruffled his hair, and with it came a whisper. His head snapped up, his gaze darting around the empty deck of the Harbinger.

"Hello?" he called out.

Silence answered him, broken only by the gentle lapping of waves. He was losing it, hearing things that weren't there.

The wind picked up again, and this time the whisper was clearer. It sounded like his name, a soft "Pete" carried on the breeze. He spun around, heart racing, but found nothing but empty air.

"It's just the wind," he muttered to himself, gripping the railing until his knuckles turned white. "Just the wind playing tricks."

He fumbled in his pocket for his phone, desperate to hear a real voice, but the screen remained stubbornly dark. Dead battery. Wouldn't work out here anyway. He tossed it aside with a curse, the clatter as it hit the deck making him jump. He went below to the cabin.

The whispers came again, a little louder this time. He couldn't make out the words, but the sound sent a chill down his spine. It reminded him of something, a memory he couldn't quite grasp.

"Shut up!" he shouted, slamming his fist against the wall.

The pain brought a moment of clarity, and he breathed deeply.

"You're okay, Pete. You're okay."

He found the journal wedged between two cushions and flipped it open with shaking hands. The pages were filled with his increasingly erratic handwriting, detailing the storm, the albatross, his growing fear. He grabbed a pen.

Day... I don't know. I'm hearing things. Whispers on the wind. It's nothing. Has to be nothing. But they sound so real.

As if summoned by his words, the whispers returned. His pen froze mid-sentence, his body tensing as he listened. This time, he could almost make out words.

"Pete... come... home..."

The pen clattered to the floor. That voice. It sounded like Jennifer. But it couldn't be. She was back in Frederiksted, probably wondering where he was. Unless...

He ran back up to the deck, his eyes scanning in all directions.

"Jen?" he called out, his voice cracking. "Jen, is that you?"

The wind whipped around him, carrying fragments of whispers. Some sounded like Jennifer, others like his father, and still others he couldn't identify. He spun in circles, trying to pinpoint the source, but the voices seemed to come from everywhere and nowhere at once.

"This isn't real," he muttered, pressing his palms against his ears. "You're hallucinating, Pete. Get it together."

But the whispers persisted, growing louder and more distinct. He could hear snippets of conversations, arguments he'd had with Jennifer, lectures from his father. He squeezed his eyes shut, willing the voices to stop, but they only grew more insistent.

When he opened his eyes, the albatross was there, circling overhead. Its presence seemed to amplify the whispers, turning them into a racket of sound that threatened to overwhelm him.

He stumbled to the helm and gripped the wheel. He had to move, had to get away from the voices. The engine roared to life, and he pushed the throttle forward, not caring which direction he was going as long as it was away from here.

The boat cut through the waves, but the whispers followed. They seemed to be coming from the water now, rising up from the depths to taunt him. He thought he caught a glimpse of a face in the foam, but it was gone before he could be sure.

"Leave me alone!" he screamed into the wind, his voice raw and desperate. The albatross kept pace overhead, its wings barely moving

SEVEN

as it glided effortlessly above the boat.

The sun had set, leaving Pete in a twilight world of shadows and whispers. He couldn't tell how long he'd been driving or in which direction. The stars above were unfamiliar, offering no guidance.

Exhaustion began to set in, and his grip on the wheel loosened. The whispers had faded to a dull murmur, but he could still hear them, waiting at the edges of his consciousness. He knew he should stop, should try to rest, but the thought of being still, of letting the voices catch up to him, was unbearable.

So he drove on into the night, the Harbinger cutting a lonely path through the dark waters. The albatross remained a constant presence above, its silhouette barely visible against the star-filled sky. And all around, the whispers continued, a haunting melody of voices from his past and present, calling out to him across the empty sea.

A memory crashed over him like a wave. The argument with Amy had been fierce, unexpected, and left him feeling hollow.

It had started on a sunny afternoon in Frederiksted. Pete had slipped away from his office, claiming a late lunch. He met Amy at their usual spot, a secluded beach hidden from prying eyes.

Amy's hair whipped in the breeze as she paced the sand.

"You promised, Pete. You said you'd tell her."

He ran a hand through his hair, frustration etched on his face.

"It's not that simple, Amy. There's more at stake than just us."

"More at stake?" Amy's voice rose, her green eyes flashing. "What about my stake in this? I'm tired of being your dirty little secret."

The words stung. He flinched, sand packing between his toes as he took a step back.

"That's not fair. You know how complicated this is."

Amy laughed, a bitter sound that cut through the air.

"Complicated? No, Pete. Complicated is trying to build a life with someone who won't commit. Complicated is loving a man who's too afraid to choose."

"I'm not afraid," he snapped, his own temper flaring. "I'm being realistic. Do you have any idea what this would do to my practice? To Jennifer?"

"Oh, poor Jennifer," Amy mocked. "Always Jennifer. Tell me, Pete, do you even love her anymore?"

The question hung in the air, heavy and accusatory. Pete's silence was damning.

Amy's face crumpled, tears welling in her eyes.

"I can't do this anymore, Pete. I won't be your backup plan."

He reached for her, but she jerked away.

"Amy, please. You know you're not a backup plan. I love you."

"Do you?" Amy's voice was barely a whisper. "Because love shouldn't feel like this. It shouldn't hurt this much."

His chest tightened. He wanted to pull her close, to make her understand. But the words stuck in his throat.

Amy wiped her eyes, her shoulders straightening.

"I'm done waiting, Pete. Either you tell Jennifer and we start our life together, or this ends. Now."

The ultimatum hung between them, as tangible as the salt in the air. Pete's mind weighed the consequences, the potential fallout.

"I need time," he said finally, his voice hoarse.

Amy's face hardened.

"Time. Always more time. Well, I'm out of time, Pete. And I'm out of patience."

She turned, walking away. He watched her go, his feet rooted to the sand. He wanted to call out, to stop her, but fear paralyzed him.

As Amy disappeared from view, he sank to his knees, the weight of his choices crushing him. The waves lapped at the shore.

The memory faded into the dark sea all around the Harbinger. The

SEVEN

argument with Amy felt like a lifetime ago, yet the pain was still fresh. He glanced at the journal lying open beside him.

The albatross circled overhead, its presence a constant reminder of his unease. He looked up at it, wondering if the bird was as lost as he felt.

* * *

The sun's risen and set more times than I can count. Or maybe it hasn't. Time's slippery out here, like trying to hold onto a fish with bare hands.

I thought I knew why I came out here. To fish. To think. To escape. But now, I'm not sure of anything. The sea stretches in every direction, an endless blue that mocks me with its vastness. There's no land in sight, no ships, no signs of life except for that godamm bird.

The albatross. It's always there, circling overhead like a vulture waiting for its meal. I've read about sailors thinking these birds bring bad luck. Never believed in that nonsense before, but now... I'm not so sure.

I keep hearing things. Whispers on the wind, voices in the waves. At first, I thought it was just the sea playing tricks on me. But they're getting clearer, more insistent. Sometimes I think I hear Jennifer calling my name. Other times, it's Amy. And then there are voices I don't recognize at all.

My head's a mess. Memories keep flooding back, things I thought I'd forgotten or buried deep. Arguments with Jennifer, stolen moments with Amy, disappointed looks from my father. They all swirl together until I can't tell what's real and what's not.

I found a sextant on board. A few days ago. Or was it weeks? I don't remember packing it, don't even know how to use the damn thing. But there it was, sitting on the deck like it had always been there. The strangest part? It looked ancient, like something you'd find in a museum. How did it get here?

The storm... God, the storm. I thought it would tear the boat apart. Waves as tall as buildings, wind that screamed like a banshee. I'm amazed I survived. But did I? Sometimes I wonder if I'm actually dead, if this is some kind of purgatory.

My supplies are running low. The fish aren't biting anymore. It's like they know something's wrong, like they're avoiding me. And the water... I swear it's changing color. Sometimes it's the deepest turquoise I've ever seen, other times it's almost black.

I keep thinking about home. About Jennifer and her practicality, always grounding me when my thoughts ran wild. About Amy and her passion, how she made me feel alive again. About my father and his constant disapproval. I left to escape all of that, but now it's all I can think about.

The albatross is watching me write this. I can feel its eyes boring into me. What does it want? Why won't it leave me alone?

I'm fucking losing my mind out here. The isolation, the confusion, the constant presence of that bird... it's all too much. I don't know how much longer I can take this. I don't even know if anyone will ever read these words.

The whispers are getting louder now. They're calling me. I think... I think I need to go to them. Maybe they have the answers I'm looking for. Maybe they can tell me why I'm here, why that bird won't leave me alone.

I'm scared. More scared than I've ever been in my life. But I'm also... curious. What's out there in the depths? What's waiting for me?

Anyone who may find this, if I don't make it back... tell Jennifer I'm sorry. Tell Amy I never meant to hurt her.

The sea is calling. I have to answer.

Pete's hand shook as he finished the entry. He stared at the words, barely recognizing his own handwriting. The whispers grew louder, more insistent. He closed the journal and stood up, his legs unsteady beneath him. The albatross circled lower, its wings casting shadows

SEVEN

across the deck. Pete looked out at the sea, its surface now a swirling mass of colors. Something was out there, calling to him. He took a step towards the edge of the boat, drawn by an irresistible force.

Eight

Pete blinked, his foot hovering over the edge of the boat. The whispers ceased, replaced by the gentle lapping of waves against the hull. He stumbled backward, heart pounding, and collapsed onto the deck.

"Jesus Christ," he muttered, running a trembling hand through his hair. "What the hell was I thinking?"

He crawled to the side of the boat and peered over the edge. The sea had returned to its normal blue, no sign of the swirling colors he'd seen moments ago. The albatross was still there, though, circling overhead.

He dragged himself to his feet and stumbled to the small bathroom. He gripped the edges of the sink and forced himself to look in the mirror.

"Well, look at you," he said to his reflection. "You're a godamm mess, Corbin."

The man staring back at him was barely recognizable. His beard had grown wild and unkempt, his eyes sunken and bloodshot. Dark circles painted the skin beneath them, a testament to sleepless nights.

"What are you doing out here?" he asked his reflection. "Running away from your problems? How's that workin' out for ya?"

His reflection sneered back at him.

"Oh, like you're one to talk," it said. "You're the one who got us into this mess in the first place."

EIGHT

He shook his head, trying to clear the cobwebs. He was talking to himself now.

Great. Just fucking great.

"Ya know, maybe Dad was right," he continued, unable to stop the words from spilling out. "Maybe I am a damn disappointment. Couldn't even manage to keep my marriage together without screwing everything up."

His reflection's eyes seemed to soften for a moment.

"But Amy…" it whispered.

"Amy?" Pete laughed bitterly. "Yeah, that was real smart. Throw away everything for what? A few moments of excitement? Some cheap thrills? Great sex, though!"

He turned on the faucet, splashing cold water on his face. When he looked up again, his reflection seemed to be smirking.

"But you enjoyed it, didn't you?" it taunted. "The secrecy, the passion. Made you feel alive again."

He slammed his fist against the mirror, not hard enough to break it, but enough to send a jolt of pain through his hand.

"Shut up," he growled. "Just shut the hell up."

He stumbled out of the bathroom, desperate to escape his own thoughts. But there was nowhere to go. The boat felt claustrophobic, the sea a prison rather than an escape.

"What am I doing?" he asked the empty air. "What the hell am I doing out here?"

The albatross cried out, as if in answer. He looked up at it, squinting against the sun.

"You got any bright ideas, bird? 'Cause I'm fresh out."

He slumped down onto the deck, back against the cabin wall. His mind felt like it was unraveling, thoughts and memories tangling together into an incomprehensible mess. He could almost hear Jennifer's voice, practical and steady, telling him to pull himself together. But then Amy's laughter would cut through, wild and carefree, urging him to let go.

And underneath it all, his father's disapproving grunt. Always judging, always finding him wanting.

"I'm losing my damn mind," he whispered to himself. "I'm actually losing my godamm mind out here."

He looked out at the endless expanse of water, feeling smaller and more insignificant than ever before. The albatross circled overhead, a constant reminder of the bad luck that seemed to follow him wherever he went.

He closed his eyes, trying to shut out the world, but the voices in his head only grew louder. He was adrift in more ways than one, lost at sea both literally and figuratively. And he had no idea how to find his way back to shore.

He squinted up at the sky, shielding his eyes from the glare of the sun. The albatross was still there, circling overhead like a vulture. He frowned, rubbing his eyes. Was it his imagination, or did the bird look... *bigger*?

He shook his head, trying to clear the cobwebs. Lack of sleep and proper food was messing with his mind. Birds didn't just grow larger. It was probably just closer, that's all.

He turned away, busying himself with checking his dwindling supplies. He'd need to start rationing soon if he didn't find his way back to land. As he rummaged through the cooler, he couldn't shake the feeling of being watched.

Against his better judgment, he looked up again. The albatross was still there, its wings spread wide against the cloudless sky. Pete's breath caught in his throat. It was definitely larger now, its wingspan easily twice what it had been before.

"That's impossible," he muttered, his voice hoarse. "You're seeing

EIGHT

things, Corbin. Get a grip."

But no matter how many times he blinked or rubbed his eyes, the albatross remained stubbornly, impossibly large. Its shadow seemed to cover half the boat now, and he could swear he heard the beating of its wings, like the rhythmic thumping of a massive heart.

The bird's size now was truly monstrous. Its beak alone looked large enough to snap the mast in two. Its eyes, once tiny pinpricks in the distance, now gleamed with an unsettling intelligence.

His breath came in short, sharp gasps. He pressed his palms against his eyes, counting to ten, willing the world to make sense again when he looked.

One... two... three...

Four... five... six...

He could hear the beating of wings, louder now, like thunder.

Seven... eight... nine...

His heart threatened to burst from his chest.

Ten.

He lowered his hands and opened his eyes. For a moment, hope flared in his chest. The sky was empty, nothing but endless blue.

Then a shadow fell over the boat, and his blood ran cold. Slowly, he turned around.

The albatross filled his entire view now, its massive eye peering at him. He stumbled backward, a strangled cry escaping his lips. This wasn't possible. Birds didn't grow to the size of houses. They didn't stare at you with eyes full of judgment and accusation.

Yet there it was, real as the boat beneath his feet, as real as the terror coursing through his veins. The albatross opened its beak, and Pete braced himself for a screech that would shatter the Harbinger's windows.

He pressed his palms against his ears and closed his eyes tight and waited.

Nothing.

He slowly opened his eyes to find the albatross was its normal size again, circling high above the boat... as before.

In that moment, He knew with absolute certainty that he had gone completely, irrevocably mad.

* * *

I still have no clue what day it is.

There's an albatross following the boat. At least, I think it's an albatross. It's been circling overhead for days now, never leaving, never resting. Sometimes I swear it's watching me.

I remember reading about albatrosses in school. Sailors used to think they were bad luck. Maybe they were onto something.

It's not just that it's following me. It's... changing. One minute it's normal-sized, the next it's as big as the damn boat. I know that's impossible. Birds don't just grow and shrink like that. But I swear I'm not making this up.

Am I losing my mind out here? Maybe the isolation is getting to me. Or maybe it's the guilt. Jennifer. Amy. They're probably worried sick about me. Or maybe they're not. Maybe they're glad I'm gone.

But this albatross... it feels like more than just a bird. Like it knows something. Like it's judging me.

I keep thinking about that poem. What was it called? Something about an Ancient Mariner. The sailor shoots an albatross and his whole crew dies. Is that what's happening to me? Am I being punished for something?

I can't shake the feeling that this bird is trying to tell me something. Or show me something. But what?

Every time I look at it, I feel this... weight. Like all my mistakes are piling up on my shoulders. Jennifer's face when I told her I was leaving. Amy's

EIGHT

tears.

Is that what the albatross means? My sins coming back to haunt me?

I don't know how much longer I can take this. The bird, the sea, the loneliness. It's all closing in on me. I keep hoping I'll wake up and this will all have been some crazy dream. But every morning, there it is. Circling. Watching. Waiting.

What does it want from me? What am I supposed to do?

I'm scared. Not just of the bird, or of being lost at sea. I'm scared of what's happening to my mind. Am I going crazy? Or am I finally seeing things clearly for the first time?

I don't know how this ends. But I have a feeling that albatross is the key to everything. I just wish I knew what it was trying to tell me.

He stopped writing, his hand cramping from gripping the pen so tightly. He stared at the words on the page, half-expecting them to rearrange themselves into some hidden message... or at least something that made any sense. But they remained stubbornly unchanged, a testament to his fractured state of mind.

He closed the journal and looked up at the sky. The albatross was still there. For a moment, He thought he saw it nod at him, as if acknowledging his attempt to understand.

But that was crazy. Birds didn't nod. They didn't grow to impossible sizes. They didn't judge.

Did they...?

Nine

Pete leaned over the railing of the Harbinger, his eyes fixed on the churning waters below.

At first, he thought it was just a trick of the light. A flash of scales beneath the surface, too large to be any fish he'd ever encountered. He blinked, rubbed his eyes, but the image persisted.

Then he saw it clearly. A massive, serpentine form undulating through the water. Its body was easily as long as his boat, and the Harbinger was a 43 footer. It was covered in iridescent scales that shimmered with an otherworldly glow. As it moved, he could make out fins that looked more like wings, propelling the creature through the water with grace.

"Jesus Christ," he muttered, his voice barely above the sound of the lapping waves. He'd heard tales of sea monsters from old salts at the marina, but he'd always dismissed them as drunken ramblings. Now, he wasn't so sure.

The creature disappeared beneath the waves, leaving him to question his own sanity. But before he could fully process what he'd seen, something else caught his eye.

In the distance, a group of what looked like *mermaids* breached the surface. Their upper bodies were unmistakably human, but where legs should have been, powerful fish tails propelled them through the water. They moved with fluid grace, their hair streaming behind them like

NINE

seaweed.

Pete's mind began to spin. This couldn't be real.

Fucking Mermaids don't exist.

Yet there they were, as clear as day, diving and surfacing in a mesmerizing dance.

One of the mermaids turned and looked directly at him. Her eyes were impossibly large and luminous, seeming to peer right into his soul. She smiled, revealing teeth that were just a bit too sharp to be human.

Pete stumbled backward, nearly tripping over a coil of rope on the deck. He closed his eyes tight, once again counting to ten before opening them again. The mermaids were gone, but the memory of those piercing eyes remained.

Just as he was about to convince himself it had all been a hallucination, something massive broke the surface of the water. At first, he thought it was a whale, but as more of it emerged, he realized it was something far stranger.

It was a giant octopus, its body easily the size of a house. But instead of the usual eight tentacles, this creature had dozens, maybe hundreds, each one writhing and twisting in the air. Its skin shifted colors rapidly, going from deep purple to electric blue to a red so vivid it hurt Pete's eyes to look at it.

The octopus's enormous eye, as big as a car tire, swiveled to focus on Pete. There was an intelligence there that terrified him, a sense of ancient wisdom and alien thought processes that his mind couldn't begin to comprehend.

One of the tentacles rose out of the water, reaching towards the Harbinger. He watched, paralyzed with fear and fascination, as it drew closer and closer. He could see the individual suckers, each one big enough to engulf his entire body.

Just as the tentacle was about to make contact with the boat, the octopus submerged, disappearing as quickly as it had appeared. The sea was left calm and empty, as if nothing had happened.

He stood there, his heart pounding in his chest, sweat beading on his forehead. He looked around wildly, half-expecting to see more creatures emerging from the depths.

But there was nothing. Just the great expanse of the sea, the cry of distant seagulls, and the ever-present albatross circling overhead.

He slumped to the deck, his back against the cabin wall. He ran a shaking hand through his hair, trying to make sense of what he'd just witnessed. Were these visions real? Had the sea truly revealed its hidden wonders to him? Or was his mind finally cracking under the strain of isolation and guilt?

He looked up at the albatross, half-expecting it to transform into some mythical beast. But it remained stubbornly, infuriatingly normal, circling endlessly as it had for days.

He closed his eyes, breathed in deep, and tried to steady himself. When he opened them again, the sea was just the sea. No monsters, no mermaids, no giant octopuses. Just water stretching to the horizon in every direction.

But he still had the feeling that beneath the surface, in the unknowable depths, those strange creatures were still there. Watching. Waiting. And maybe, just maybe… judging him as harshly as he judged himself.

* * *

Pete looked out at the horizon, his eyes burning from the relentless sun and lack of sleep. For a moment, he thought he saw something—a smudge of green against the blue. He blinked, rubbed his eyes, and looked again.

NINE

There it was.

An island!

His heart leapt. Could it be? Had he finally found land after days of aimless drifting? He scrambled to his feet, nearly losing his balance on the gently rocking deck of the Harbinger.

The island seemed to shimmer in the distance, like a mirage in a desert. Lush palm trees swayed in a breeze he couldn't feel. He could almost hear the rustle of their fronds, smell the sweet scent of tropical flowers.

"It's real," he muttered to himself. "It's gotta be real."

He fumbled for the boat's controls, his hands shaking with excitement and exhaustion. The engine sputtered to life, and he aimed the Harbinger towards the beckoning shore.

As he drew closer, details began to emerge. A pristine white beach stretched along the island's edge, the sand looking soft enough to sink into. Behind the beach, a dense jungle rose up, promising shade and shelter. He could see colorful birds flitting between the trees, their plumage a riot of reds and blues against the green backdrop.

He laughed, a sound that surprised him with its unfamiliarity. How long had it been since he'd laughed? Since before he set out on this ill-fated trip.

The island was close now, so close he could almost reach out and touch it. He could see a natural harbor, perfect for mooring the Harbinger. He imagined himself stepping onto that beach, feeling solid ground beneath his feet again. He'd find fresh water, food, maybe even other people.

But as the Harbinger approached the island's shore, something strange began to happen. The edges of the island seemed to blur, like a watercolor painting left out in the rain. The vibrant colors began to fade, washing out to pale imitations of themselves.

He blinked hard, shook his head. When he looked again, the island was even less distinct. The trees looked more like rough sketches than real objects. The beach was a vague suggestion of white rather than the inviting stretch of sand he'd seen moments ago.

"No," he whispered, his voice cracking. "Fuck No."

He pushed the throttle forward, urging the Harbinger on. But with each passing second, the island became less and less real. The birds disappeared first, winking out of existence like snuffed candles. Then the jungle faded away, leaving only the faintest outline of trees.

He watched in horror as the beach dissolved before his eyes, melting into the sea like sugar in hot coffee. The last to go was the natural harbor, its protective arms seeming to reach out towards him before they, too, vanished.

And then, just like that, the island was gone. He was left staring at an empty horizon, the endless blue of sea meeting sky with no break in between.

He cut the engine, letting the Harbinger drift to a stop. For a long moment, he just stood there, gripping the wheel so tightly his knuckles were white.

He slumped to the deck. He buried his face in his hands, fighting back tears of frustration and despair. When he looked up again, the sea spread out before him, vast and empty and indifferent to his plight... as always.

The albatross circled. He glared up at it, half-wishing he had a gun to shoot the damned thing out of the sky.

"You saw it too, didn't you?" he called out to the bird. "Tell me you saw it."

The albatross offered no response, continuing its perpetual flight as if Pete didn't exist at all.

* * *

NINE

Pete sat on the deck, still feeling defeated by the disappearance of the island. As he stared out at the water, the sun's harsh glare softened, and the salty sea air transformed into the crisp scent of autumn leaves.

He found himself transported back to a crisp October afternoon in his childhood. The memory enveloped him like a warm blanket, momentarily shielding him from the harsh reality of his current situation.

Little Pete, no more than eight years old, scampered through a field of pumpkins, his father's deep laughter echoing behind him. The pumpkin patch stretched as far as his young eyes could see, a sea of orange dotted with vibrant greens and browns.

"Hold up there, champ," his father called out, his voice lacking its usual stern edge. "We gotta find the perfect one for your ma."

Pete slowed his pace, turning to watch his father navigate the uneven ground between the pumpkins. Jonathon Corbin, usually so imposing in his suit and tie, looked almost comical in his old flannel shirt and muddy boots.

"How about this one, Dad?" Pete pointed to a misshapen pumpkin with a lumpy exterior.

Jonathon chuckled, ruffling Pete's hair.

"That's a fine choice if we're aiming to scare the neighbors. But let's keep lookin', shall we?"

They wandered through the patch, Pete occasionally stumbling over a vine or tripping on his untied shoelaces. Each time, his father's strong hands were there to catch him, accompanied by a gentle reminder to watch his step.

As the afternoon wore on, the air grew cooler, and the sky painted itself in hues of orange and pink. Pete's enthusiasm began to wane, his earlier boundless energy giving way to fatigue.

"Tell ya what," Jonathon said, noticing his son's drooping shoulders. "How about we take a break? I brought along somethin' special."

From his backpack, he produced a thermos and two mugs. The rich aroma of hot chocolate filled the air as he poured, steam rising in delicate wisps.

Pete cupped the mug in his small hands, savoring the warmth. He took a careful sip, the sweet taste of chocolate mingling with a hint of cinnamon – his mother's secret recipe.

"This is the best hot chocolate ever," he declared, a chocolate mustache adorning his upper lip.

Jonathon laughed, a sound free from the weight of expectations and disappointments that would color their later years.

"Don't let your mother hear ya say that. She'll start thinkin' I can cook."

As they sat among the pumpkins, sipping their hot chocolate, Jonathon pointed to the sky.

"Look there, Pete. See that group of stars? That's Orion, the hunter."

Pete followed his father's finger, his eyes wide with wonder.

"Wow," he breathed. "How do you know that, Dad?"

"My father taught me," Jonathon said, his voice soft with nostalgia. "And now I'm teaching you. That's how it goes, son. We pass down what we know, hoping our children will carry it forward."

In that moment, surrounded by pumpkins and bathed in the glow of twilight, he felt a connection to his father that transcended their usual roles. Here, they were just a man and a boy, sharing hot chocolate and stargazing.

As the memory began to fade, adult Pete found himself reaching out, trying to hold onto that feeling of warmth and connection. But like the mirage of the island, it slipped through his fingers, leaving him once again alone on the deck of the Harbinger.

The albatross circled overhead, a constant reminder of his current reality. Yet, for a brief moment, he felt a flicker of comfort. The memory, though bittersweet, had provided a temporary respite from

NINE

his despair.

He closed his eyes, trying to recapture the scent of autumn leaves and hot chocolate. When he opened them again, he was met with the endless blue of the sea and sky. But somewhere deep inside, a small spark of warmth remained, a reminder of a time when the world seemed full of wonder and his father's love felt unconditional.

Ten

The memory of meeting Amy for the first time flooded Pete's mind, and he began to write in his journal, his pen scratching across the paper.

I remember the day I met Amy like it was yesterday. Christ, was it really only six months ago? It was at that stupid fundraiser Jennifer dragged me to. I didn't wanna go, but she insisted it'd be good for my practice. 'Networking,' she called it. What a load of shit.

I was standin' there, bored outta my mind, when this whirlwind of a woman crashed into me. Literally crashed. Spilled her drink all over my new suit. I oughta have been mad, but when I looked up, I saw these green eyes that just... I dunno, they grabbed me.

'Oh my God, I'm so sorry!' she said, laughing and trying to dab at my jacket with a cocktail napkin. 'I'm such a klutz. I swear, I shouldn't be allowed in public.'

I told her it was fine, but she wouldn't let up. Kept apologizing and fussin' over me. Next thing I knew, she was draggin' me to the bar to buy me a drink as an apology. That's Amy for ya - always rushin' headlong into things without thinkin'.

We got to talkin', and boy, could she talk. One minute she's tellin' me about her job as a yoga instructor, the next she's going on about this book she read on quantum physics. Her mind was all over the place, but in a way that

TEN

was... I dunno, exciting? Made me feel alive just listenin' to her.

But there was somethin' else there too. Somethin' under all that energy and enthusiasm. Every now and then, when she thought I wasn't looking, I'd catch this look in her eyes. Like she was waitin' for the other shoe to drop. Like she couldn't quite believe I was still there, listenin' to her.

I remember thinkin', 'This girl's got layers.' Sure, she was beautiful - all long blonde hair and curves in all the right places. But it was more than that. She was like one of those Russian dolls. The ones where you open it up and there's another one inside, and another, and another.

We ended up sneakin' out of that stuffy fundraiser and going for a walk on the beach. It was her idea, of course. 'Let's get outta here,' she said, grabbin' my hand like we'd known each other for years. 'I know a place where we can see the stars.'

And just like that, I followed her. Didn't even think about Jennifer, didn't think about anythin' except Amy's hand in mine and the sound of her laugh carryin' on the night air.

We sat on the sand, and she pointed out constellations to me. Got most of 'em wrong, but I didn't have the heart to correct her. She was so damn excited about it all.

Then, outta nowhere, she turns to me and says, 'You're not like other guys, are you, Pete?' And before I could answer, she kissed me. Just like that. No hesitation, no askin' permission. Just pure Amy.

But after, when she pulled away, I saw it again. That flash of insecurity in her eyes. Like she was waitin' for me to push her away or tell her off. When I didn't, when I kissed her back instead, it was like... I dunno, like a light went on inside her.

I knew right then I was in trouble. Knew I should've walked away, gone back to the fundraiser, back to Jennifer. But I didn't. Couldn't. Amy was like a force of nature, and I got swept up in her.

Looking back now, I wonder if I saw what I wanted to see in her. If I was so caught up in the excitement and the newness that I ignored the warning signs. But hell, maybe that's just hindsight talkin'.

All I know is, that night changed everything. And now here I am, stuck on this godamm boat, thinkin' about Amy and Jennifer and the mess I've made of everything. Christ, what a joke.

He stopped writing, his hand cramping from gripping the pen too tightly. He stared at the words on the page, feeling a mix of guilt and longing wash over him. The memory of that night with Amy was so vivid… so alive.

* * *

Jesus, how'd I end up here? Successful psychiatrist, they call me. What a joke. If they only knew…

He paused, tapping the pen against the page, then continued:

I remember when I first decided to become a shrink. Dad was so disappointed. 'A real man works with his hands,' he'd say. Like bein' a doctor wasn't good enough for him. But I wanted to help people. Thought I could make a difference.

And for a while, I did. I was good at it, too. People opened up to me. I could see right through their bullshit, help 'em sort out their problems. But somewhere along the line, things changed.

Maybe it was the pressure. Everyone comin' to me with their problems, day in and day out. It's like… it's like they were all drowning, and I was the only lifeguard on duty. And after a while, you start to feel like you're drownin' too.

Jennifer didn't get it. She'd say, 'It's just a job, Pete. Leave it at the office.'

TEN

But how could I? These were people's lives I was dealin' with. Their hopes, their fears, their deepest secrets. You can't just switch that off.

I started stayin' later at the office, takin' on more patients. Thought if I could just help one more person, make one more breakthrough, it'd all be worth it. But it was never enough.

The more I helped others, the more I felt like I was losin' myself. Started havin' trouble sleepin'. Couldn't turn my brain off. All those stories, all that pain... it was like it was seeping into me.

And then there was the pressure to keep up appearances. The successful Dr. Corbin, always put together, always in control. Ha! If they could see me now...

I started drinkin' more. Just to take the edge off, I told myself. But it wasn't enough. Nothing was ever enough.

That's when I met Amy. She was... different. Didn't expect anythin' from me. Didn't need me to fix her. With her, I could just... be.

But that only made things worse, didn't it? Now I was lyin' to Jennifer, sneakin' around. The guilt was eatin' me alive. But I couldn't stop. It was like I was watchin' myself from the outside, makin' all these stupid decisions, but I couldn't do anythin' about it.

And all the while, the patients kept comin'. More problems, more pain. I was supposed to have all the answers, but I couldn't even figure out my own life.

So I ran. Got on this boat and just... left. Thought maybe if I could get away from it all, I could clear my head. Figure things out.

But now I'm lost in more ways than one. Lost at sea, lost in my own head. And I'm startin' to think maybe there's no way back.

* * *

The sun was setting now. Pete continued:

Had the strangest dream last night. Can't shake it.

I was back home in Frederiksted, standin' on the beach. It was night, but the moon was so bright it might as well have been day. The water was calm, like glass. I could see my reflection in it, clear as anything.

Then I heard Jennifer callin' my name. She was out there in the water, wavin' at me. I started walkin' towards her, but the water... it was weird. It didn't feel wet. It was like walkin' on air.

I kept goin', tryin' to reach her. But the farther I went, the farther away she seemed. And then I heard another voice. Amy. She was callin' me too, from the opposite direction.

I turned around, and there she was, standin' on the shore where I'd just been. She looked scared, like she needed my help.

I didn't know what to do. I was stuck there, in the middle of the ocean, with Jennifer in one direction and Amy in the other. And then I realized I couldn't move. My feet were stuck.

I looked down, and the water wasn't water anymore. It was like... quicksand or somethin'. It was pullin' me down.

I tried to yell for help, but no sound came out. Jennifer and Amy, they both disappeared. And then I saw my old man, standin' on a boat nearby. He was just watchin' me, shakin' his head. Disappointment written all over his face, same as always.

The... whatever it was, it was up to my chest now. I could feel it pressin' in on me, makin' it hard to breathe. And all the while, Dad just stood there, watchin'.

Just before it covered my face, I heard him say, "You made your bed, Pete. Now you gotta lie in it."

And then I was under. But I could still see. All around me were faces. My patients. Hundreds of 'em, all starin' at me with these... accusing eyes. Like they knew. Knew all the things I'd done, all the ways I'd failed 'em.

TEN

I tried to swim, to fight my way back up, but it was like my limbs wouldn't work. Then, Amy appeared in the water with me, only she wasn't submerged like me... she was holding me under the water and she had an evil grin on her face. Somehow, through the water or whatever it had become, I could hear her saying, "You deserve this, Pete! You put us in this place!" And the whole time, in the background, I could hear this... sound. Like a bird screechin'. It got louder and louder until it was all I could hear.

I woke up gaspin' for air, covered in sweat. Took me a minute to remember where I was. That damn albatross was circlin' overhead, screamin' like it knew what I'd been dreamin' about.

Fuck, what's happenin' to me? I came out here to clear my head, but it's like... it's like all the shit I was runnin' from followed me. Can't escape it, even in my sleep.

Maybe Dad was right. Maybe I did make my bed. But how the hell am I supposed to lie in it when I'm out here in the middle of nowhere? When I can't even trust my own mind anymore?

That dream... it felt so real. Like I was really drownin'. And Amy? What was that about? Maybe I am drownin'. Maybe I've been drownin' for years and just didn't want to admit it.

I keep thinkin' about all those faces. My patients. What would they think if they could see me now? Their doctor, the one who's supposed to have all the answers, lost at sea, talkin' to himself and jumpin' at shadows.

And Jennifer and Amy... God, what a mess I've made. Tryin' to keep 'em both happy, and in the end, I'm just hurtin' everyone. Including myself.

I don't know how to fix this. Don't even know if I can. But I know I can't keep goin' like this. Somethin's gotta give.

That screechin'... I can still hear it. Even when that damn bird isn't making a sound. It's like it's in my head now. Won't leave me alone.

I'm scared. Never thought I'd admit that, even to myself. But I am. Scared of what's happenin' to me. Scared I might not make it back. Scared of what I'll face if I do.

Maybe that's what the dream was about. Maybe I'm already drownin', and this... this is just my mind's way of lettin' me know.

* * *

Jenny,

I don't know if you'll ever read this. Hell, I don't know if I'll ever see you again. But I gotta write this down, even if it's just for me.

I'm sorry. God, I'm so fucking sorry. For everything. For being a lousy husband, for not appreciating you, for... well, you know. I've been sittin' out here, thinkin' about all the ways I screwed up, and it's like a damn avalanche. One thing after another.

Remember when we first met? At that stupid frat party? You were wearin' that green dress, and I thought you were the most beautiful girl I'd ever seen. Still do, you know. Even after all these years.

I keep thinkin' about all the little moments. The way you scrunch up your nose when you're concentratin'. How you always burn the toast but pretend you meant to do it. The sound of your laugh when you're really, truly happy.

I miss that laugh, Jenny. I miss you.

I know I haven't been the man you deserve. I've been selfish, caught up in my own bullshit. Thinkin' about my career, about... other things. But out here, with nothin' but the sea and sky, I realize what really matters.

You matter, Jenny. You always have.

I wish I could go back. Change things. Be the man you thought I was when you married me. But I can't. All I can do is sit here and hope I get another chance.

If I do... if I make it back... I swear I'll do better. I'll be better. For you. For us.

I love you, Jenny. Always have, always will. Even when I was too stupid

TEN

to show it.

I hope you can forgive me. I'm tryin' to forgive myself, but it ain't easy.

If I don't make it back... just know that my last thoughts were of you. Of the life we could've had if I hadn't been such a godamm fool.

I love you. I'm sorry. I hope that's enough.

Pete

He hadn't been this honest with himself—or with Jenny—in years. It felt good to get it out, but it also made the weight of his mistakes feel even heavier.

He closed the journal, running his hand over the worn cover. Part of him wanted to tear out the page, to throw it into the sea and pretend he'd never written it. But he couldn't. It was the truth, maybe the first real truth he'd faced in a long time.

He tucked the journal away, safe from the spray of the sea. Maybe Jenny would read it someday. Maybe she wouldn't. But at least he'd said what needed saying, even if it was too late.

Eleven

Pete's eyes snapped open. He'd dozed off again, slumped against the wheel of the Harbinger. How long had he been out? Minutes? Hours? The concept of time had become as fluid as the sea around him.

He rubbed his eyes, trying to shake off the fog of exhaustion. That's when he heard it. A soft thud from below deck.

He froze, his hand hovering in front of his face. He held his breath, straining his ears. There it was again. A shuffling sound, like someone moving around in the cabin.

"Hello?" he called out.

No answer came, just the creaking of the boat and the lapping of waves against the hull.

He shook his head. He was imagining things. Had to be. He was alone out here, miles from anywhere. But as he started to relax, he heard it again. Clearer this time. Footsteps.

"Who's there?" he shouted, grabbing a fishing rod as a makeshift weapon.

Silence answered him.

He inched towards the cabin door, his heart hammering so loud he was sure whoever—or whatever—was down there could hear it. He reached for the handle, hesitated, then yanked the door open.

Nothing. The cabin was empty, just as he'd left it. Clothes strewn about, empty food wrappers, his duffel bag in the corner. But something felt off. It almost seemed like things had been moved, ever so slightly.

He stepped inside, eyes darting around the small space. The air felt different, heavier somehow. Like someone had been breathing in it recently.

"I know you're here," he said, trying to keep his voice steady. "Come out now, and we can talk about this."

A soft chuckle echoed through the cabin, seeming to come from everywhere and nowhere at once. He spun around, rod raised, but there was no one there.

"Who are you?" he demanded, panic rising in his throat. "What do you want?"

The laughter came again, closer this time. Right behind him. He whirled around, swinging the rod wildly. It connected with nothing but air.

He stumbled backwards, out of the cabin and onto the deck. The sun was setting and casting eerie shadows across the boat. Shadows that seemed to move and shift in ways they shouldn't.

He was losing it. Had to be. There was no one else here. It was just his mind playing tricks on him.

But then he saw it. A figure, just at the edge of his vision. When he turned to look at it, it vanished. But he could feel its presence, watching him.

"Leave me alone!" he screamed, spinning in circles, trying to catch a glimpse of his tormentor. "Get off my fucking boat!"

He scanned the deck. The figure he'd seen—or thought he'd seen—had vanished, but he couldn't shake the feeling of being watched.

He gripped the fishing rod tighter.

"Come out, you bastard," he muttered through clenched teeth.

Starting at the bow, he began a methodical search of the Harbinger.

He checked behind every crate, peered into every crevice. The boat wasn't the biggest boat in the world, but there were plenty of hiding spots for someone determined to stay hidden.

He moved to the port side, checking the lifeboats. Nothing but empty seats and coiled rope. The starboard side yielded similar results. His frustration grew with each empty space he encountered.

Back at the stern, he paused. The engine compartment. He hadn't checked there yet. It was a tight squeeze, but someone could potentially hide there if they were desperate enough.

He hesitated, his hand hovering over the hatch. Did he really want to open it? What if something was waiting for him down there?

"Don't be a godamm coward," he scolded himself. With a deep breath, he yanked the hatch open.

The smell of oil and diesel fuel wafted up. He peered into the darkness, half-expecting to see a pair of eyes staring back at him. But there was nothing. Just the usual tangle of pipes and machinery.

He slammed the hatch shut, cursing under his breath. Where the hell was this thing hiding?

He stormed back to the cabin, determined to tear the place apart if necessary. He ripped open cabinets, tossed aside cushions, even checked inside the tiny bathroom. Nothing.

As he stood in the middle of the now-ransacked cabin, He felt a chill. He slowly turned around, half-expecting to see the figure standing behind him. But the doorway was empty.

He ran a hand through his hair, his mind racing. He'd searched every inch of the boat. There was nowhere left for anyone—or anything—to hide. Which meant…

"I'm losing my fucking mind," he whispered.

* * *

ELEVEN

Pete huddled in the corner of the cabin, his back pressed against the wall. The night had brought with it a symphony of sounds that tormented him relentlessly. Whispers drifted through the air, unintelligible yet unmistakably there. He clamped his hands over his ears, but it did nothing to drown out the noise.

"Shut up, shut up, shut up," he muttered, rocking back and forth.

A faint melody wafted through the cabin, a hauntingly familiar tune he couldn't quite place. He squeezed his eyes shut, trying to mentally block it out, but the music only seemed to grow louder.

Then he heard it—his own voice, arguing with someone just outside the cabin door. He froze, listening intently.

"You can't do this," his disembodied voice said. "It's not right."

"Since when do you care about what's right?" another voice responded. It sounded like his father, but that was impossible. Of course, so was his *own* voice being heard.

He scrambled to his feet. He grabbed a chair and wedged it under the doorknob, barricading himself inside. His eyes darted around the cabin, searching for anything else he could use to fortify his position.

No one's getting in here, he thought. *No one's out there. It's all in your head, Pete. All in your head.*

But even as he said it, he didn't believe it. The voices outside continued their heated argument, growing louder and more intense with each passing moment.

He paced the small confines of the cabin, running his hands through his hair. He needed to think, needed to figure out what was happening to him. But his thoughts were a jumbled mess, scattered by fear and confusion.

A new scent cut through the musty air of the cabin—a familiar perfume that made his stomach lurch.

Amy's perfume.

He could almost feel her presence, as if she were standing right behind him.

"Amy?" he whispered, turning around.

But the cabin was empty save for him and his growing terror.

The perfume lingered, mixing with the sounds that assaulted him from all sides. He sank to the floor, overwhelmed by the sensory onslaught. He curled into a ball, trying to make himself as small as possible.

"It's not real," he repeated to himself, over and over. "None of it's real."

But real or not, the torment continued throughout the long, hellish night. He remained huddled on the floor, trapped between the imaginary intruders outside and the very real demons in his own mind.

* * *

The pen skittered across the paper, leaving jagged lines and smudges in its wake.

They're watching me. I can feel their eyes boring into my skull. Every time I turn around, I catch a glimpse of something darting out of sight. It's driving me crazy.

He paused, taking a shaky breath, and glanced over his shoulder, half-expecting to see someone—or something—standing there.

It's not just the albatross anymore. That damn bird is still out there, circling overhead like some kind of flying demon waiting for me to die. But now there's more. Shadows moving at the edge of my vision. The whispers...

ELEVEN

He rubbed his eyes, trying to clear his vision. He hadn't slept in... how long? He couldn't remember. The days had begun to blur together, an endless cycle of paranoia and fear.

I tried to radio for help again today. All I got was static and... something else. A voice, I think. But not human. It was all garbled and distorted, like it was coming from underwater. It kept repeating something over and over, but I couldn't make out the words.

He looked up from the journal, his gaze drawn to the cabin window.

I ask again, am I losing my mind? Maybe I've already lost it. How else can I explain what's happening? The creatures I've seen in the water. The island that appeared and disappeared like a mirage. And now these... whatever they are.

Pete's writing became even more erratic, the words barely legible.

They're not just watching anymore. I can feel them. Their presence. I can't escape it. Even when I close my eyes, I know they're there. Waiting. Watching. But for what?

He slammed the journal shut, unable to write anymore. He pressed his back against the wall, eyes darting around the cabin.

"I know you're there," he whispered, his voice hoarse. "What do you want from me?"

Only silence answered him. But in that silence, He could have sworn he heard the faintest sound of laughter.

A woman's laughter...

Twelve

Pete rubbed his face, trying to shake off the fog of exhaustion. As he lowered his hands, something caught his eye through the cabin window. A figure, pale and translucent, stood on the deck.

He blinked hard, certain his mind was playing tricks on him again. But when he looked back, the figure was still there. It was a man, tall and lean, with a weather-beaten face and eyes that seemed to hold the depths of the very sea he was on.

"Grandpa?" he whispered.

The ghostly figure turned, looking at him. A sad smile played across its lips, and Pete was transported back in time.

This time, he was ten years, sitting on the dock next to his grandfather. The old man's gnarled hands worked deftly, showing Pete how to tie a fisherman's knot.

"Remember, Petey," his grandfather said, his voice gravelly but kind, "the sea doesn't give up her secrets easily. You gotta earn 'em."

Young Pete nodded solemnly, his small fingers fumbling with the rope.

"Is that why Dad doesn't like the sea?"

His grandfather chuckled.

"Your father likes the sea fine… but he's a man of business, not pleasure. Always has been. But you, my boy, you've got salt water

TWELVE

in your veins."

Pete looked up at his grandfather, confusion etched on his face.

"What does that mean?"

The old man's eyes twinkled.

"It means the sea calls to ya, just like it called to me. It's in your blood."

"Is that a good thing?" Pete asked, still struggling with the knot.

His grandfather was quiet for a moment, gazing out at the horizon.

"It can be," he finally said. "The sea can give you freedom like nothing else. But it can take, too. You gotta respect it, Petey. Never forget that."

Pete found himself back in the cabin, staring at the ghostly figure on the deck. It hadn't moved, those familiar eyes still fixed on him.

"I remember, Grandpa," he murmured. "I remember."

The figure nodded slowly, then turned and walked towards the bow of the boat. Pete scrambled to his feet, nearly falling in his haste to follow. He burst out of the cabin, the cool night air hitting him like a slap.

But the deck was empty. The ghostly figure of his grandfather had vanished, leaving him alone once more. He stumbled to the railing, gripping it tightly as he scanned the darkness.

"Grandpa?" he called out, his voice swallowed by the vastness of the sea. "Grandpa, where are you?"

Only the sound of the waves answered him. He slumped against the railing. Was it real? Had he truly seen his grandfather's ghost? Or was it just another hallucination, another trick of his fractured psyche?

He looked up at the sky, searching for the albatross that had become his constant companion.

"What are you trying to tell me?" he whispered to the sky. "What am I supposed to do?"

***

I saw Grandpa tonight. Or I think I did. Christ, I don't know anymore. He was there on the deck, clear as day, but... not. Transparent, like some kinda godamm Hollywood ghost. But it felt real. It felt so damn real.

Maybe the isolation and the sea and that damn bird have finally driven me over the edge. But if I'm crazy, why did it feel so... right? Like he was really there, trying to tell me something.

We had a moment, me and ghost-Grandpa. It took me back to when I was a kid, sitting on that old dock, learning to tie knots. I remember every word he said to me that day. About having salt water in my veins, about the sea calling to me. Funny how clear that memory is, when I can barely remember what I last had for breakfast. Hell, I don't even know what day it is anymore.

But Grandpa... he always got me in a way Dad never did. He understood why I loved the sea, why I needed it. Dad always thought it was a waste of time. 'No future in chasin' fish,' he'd say. As if that's all it was about.

Grandpa knew better. He knew it was about freedom, about finding yourself out here where there's nothing but you and the water and the sky. But he warned me too, didn't he? 'The sea can take,' he said. Jesus, what if that's what he was trying to tell me tonight?

Am I in danger? Is that why he showed up? Or is this just my guilty conscience playing tricks on me? Maybe it's trying to remind me of simpler times, before I screwed everything up with Jen and Amy.

But why Grandpa? Why not Dad? Or Jen? Or even Amy? Why him? What's the significance?

'Salt water in my veins. Sea calls to me.'

Is that what's happening now? Is the sea calling me home? Christ, that sounds morbid. Like I'm destined to die out here or something.

No. No, that can't be it. I refuse to believe that. There's gotta be another explanation. Maybe... maybe it's a sign. A reminder of why I came out here

TWELVE

in the first place. To find myself again, to reconnect with that part of me that Grandpa saw all those years ago.

But then why did he look so sad? Why did he disappear when I tried to follow him? Was he disappointed in me? In what I've become?

I wish I could talk to him. Really talk to him, not just stare at some apparition on the deck. I've got so many questions, so many things I need to figure out. About my life, about my choices, about where I go from here.

Maybe that's the point. Maybe he can't give me the answers. Maybe I've gotta figure this shit out on my own.

But how? How am I supposed to do that when I can't even trust my own eyes anymore? When I'm seeing ghosts and hearing whispers and that damn albatross won't leave me alone?

I keep thinking about what Grandpa said about the sea. That it doesn't give up its secrets easily. That you gotta earn them. Is that what I'm doing out here? Earning the sea's secrets? And if so, what the hell are they?

I feel like I'm on the edge of something. Like I'm close to figuring it all out, but I can't quite grasp it. It's like trying to catch smoke with my bare hands. The more I reach for it, the more it slips away.

But I can't give up. I won't. I've come too far, lost too much to turn back now. Whatever the sea's trying to tell me, whatever Grandpa was trying to show me, I've gotta see it through.

Even if it kills me.

* * *

The deck swayed beneath Pete's feet, but he couldn't tell if it was the sea or his own unsteady mind. He blinked, rubbing his eyes, sure he was hallucinating again.

But there they were. Seated around a table that hadn't been there before, ghostly figures from his past chatted and laughed as if at some macabre dinner party.

"What the hell?" he muttered, inching closer.

His father, Jonathan, sat at the head of the table, carving into a spectral roast with precise, angry motions. Beside him, Pete's wife Jennifer sipped from an empty wine glass, her eyes distant and sad. Across from her, Amy, Pete's mistress, twirled her fork between her fingers, shooting furtive glances at the others.

And there, at the far end, was his grandfather, pipe clenched between his teeth, regarding the scene with a mixture of amusement and disappointment.

"Well, look who finally decided to join us," Jonathan's voice boomed, making Pete flinch. "The prodigal son returns."

"Dad?" Pete whispered, his voice cracking. "What… what is this?"

"Family dinner, of course," Jennifer replied, her tone icy. "You remember those, don't you? Or were you too busy with your… extracurricular activities?"

Amy shifted uncomfortably in her seat, the silverware in her hands clattering against the plate.

"Now, now," Grandpa interjected, puffing on his pipe. "Let's not air all our dirty laundry at once. We've got all night, after all."

Pete's head spun. This couldn't be real. And yet, the smell of pot roast filled the air, mingling with the salt of the sea.

"Sit down, son," Jonathan commanded, gesturing to an empty chair. "Your food's getting cold."

Hesitantly, Pete lowered himself into the seat. A plate materialized before him, piled high with his childhood favorites.

"I don't understand," he mumbled, picking up his fork. "You're all… you can't be here."

"Oh, we're here alright," Amy said, reaching across the table to touch his hand. Her fingers passed right through him, leaving a chill. "You

TWELVE

brought us here, Pete. All your secrets, all your lies... they've been festering. And now? Now it's time to face the music."

Jennifer laughed, a hollow sound.

"Face the music? That's rich, coming from you. Tell me, Amy, did you know he was married when you first *fucked* him?"

Amy's face fell, her form flickering like a candle in the wind.

"I... that's not fair. He told me—"

"He told you what he always tells people," Jonathan interrupted, sawing viciously at his meat. "Whatever they want to hear. Isn't that right, Pete? Always the smooth talker, always the charmer. But when it comes to actually following through? Well..."

His grandfather cleared his throat.

"Now, Johnny, let's not be too harsh. The boy's got his faults, sure, but—"

"Don't defend him," Jennifer snapped. "You always did, and look where it got us. Look where it got me."

The accusations flew back and forth across the table, each one striking Pete like a punch to the jaw. He wanted to argue, to defend himself, but the words stuck in his throat.

"I'm sorry," he finally managed to choke out. "I never meant... I didn't want to hurt anyone."

The table fell silent, all eyes turning to him. Even the albatross, perched on the railing behind them and seemed to be waiting for his next words.

"But you did hurt us, Pete," his father said, his voice uncharacteristically gentle. "You hurt all of us. And yourself most of all."

Pete felt tears welling up in his eyes.

"I know. God, I know. I've made such a mess of everything. I just don't... I don't know how to fix it."

His grandfather leaned forward, his pipe smoke swirling in strange patterns.

"Maybe that's the problem, boy. Maybe you've been so busy trying to fix things, you never stopped to figure out what was broken in the first place."

Pete looked around the table, really looked, for the first time. At his father's disappointment, his wife's pain, Amy's guilt. And in their faces, he saw reflections of his own failures, his own fears.

"I'm lost," he whispered, more to himself than to them. "I'm so lost."

He stared at the ghostly figures around the table. The impossibility of the situation clashed with the vivid sensations assaulting him - the smell of pot roast and cherry-vanilla pipe smoke, the clink of silverware, the familiar cadence of his father's voice.

"Remember when you were ten, and I caught you trying to sneak out to go fishing?" his father's apparition asked, a wry smile playing on his translucent lips.

Pete nodded, the memory washing over him. He could almost feel the cool grass under his bare feet, the weight of his fishing rod in his hand.

"You grounded me for a week," Pete said, his voice barely above a whisper.

His father's ghost chuckled.

"And you spent that entire week reading every fishing book in the house. Said if you couldn't fish, you'd at least learn everything about it."

The scene shifted, and Pete was standing in his childhood bedroom, surrounded by stacks of books. He could hear his younger self muttering fish names under his breath.

"You were always so determined," his mother's voice drifted from somewhere behind him. Pete turned, but she wasn't there. Only her words remained, echoing in the air.

"Mom?" he said, his voice breaking. "I've missed you so mu—"

The bedroom dissolved, replaced by the deck of his boat. But it

TWELVE

wasn't the same - this was years ago, the first time he'd taken Jennifer out on the water.

Ghost-Jennifer stood at the railing, her hair whipping in the wind.

"I fell in love with you that day," she said, not turning to look at him. "You were so passionate, so alive out here on the water. What happened to that man, Pete?"

He reached out to touch her shoulder, but his hand passed through her form. "I'm still here," he whispered, but even to his own ears, the words sounded hollow.

The scene shifted again. This time, he was in his office, surrounded by diplomas and awards. Amy sat across from him, her eyes bright with admiration.

"Dr. Corbin," ghost-Amy purred, leaning forward. "You're so accomplished, so respected. It must be nice, having everything figured out."

He wanted to laugh at the irony. If only she knew how lost he truly was.

"I never had it figured out," he admitted, more to himself than to the apparition before him. "I was just... good at pretending."

The office faded away, and he found himself back on the deck of his boat. But now, it felt different. The air was heavy with an oppressive energy, and shadows seemed to dance at the corners of his vision.

"This boat," his grandfather's voice rumbled from somewhere, "it's more than just wood and metal, isn't it, boy?"

Pete nodded, a chill running down his spine.

"It's... it's alive," he whispered, the realization hitting him. "Or... haunted."

The albatross, still perched on the railing, let out a mournful cry. Pete spun to face it, certain that it was more than just a bird. It was a *harbinger*, a messenger from some other realm.

"What are you trying to tell me?" he demanded, his voice cracking with desperation. "What do you want from me?"

But the albatross remained silent, its black beady eyes fixed on him with an unsettling intensity. Like some kind of demon.

Pete stumbled back, his legs hitting the table where the ghostly dinner party had been. But now, the table was empty, the apparitions gone. Only the oppressive feeling of being watched remained.

"This isn't real," he muttered. "It can't be real. I'm losing my mind."

But even as he said it, he knew it wasn't true. The boat creaked and groaned around him, as if agreeing with his unspoken thoughts. This was real. Too real. The ghosts, the memories, the albatross - they were all part of something bigger, something he couldn't yet understand.

He sank to his knees on the deck, overwhelmed by the weight of his realizations. The boat was haunted, yes, but not by external spirits. It was haunted by his own past, his own failures and regrets, his own sins… given form by the isolation and the unforgiving sea.

And as the night wore on, he remained there, trapped between the physical world of his boat and the spectral realm of his memories, unsure which was more real - or more dangerous.

* * *

Ever the analyzing psychiatrist, Pete needed to make sense of what he'd seen, to catalog the apparitions that had haunted his boat.

These apparitions… they're not just random. They're all connected to my past, my regrets, my failures. But the boat isn't haunted by ghosts, it's haunted by me. By my own guilt and shame.

Father represents my constant feelings of inadequacy.

Mother is the unconditional love I've lost.

TWELVE

Jennifer shows me the love I've squandered.
Amy is the embodiment of my betrayal.
Grandfather might be trying to guide me, but to what?
My younger self is a painful reminder of the man I could have been.
And the Albatross... is it death? Judgment? Or something else entirely?

I'm trapped here, not just on this boat, but between the world of the now and the world of my memories. Everything is blurring together. I can't tell what's real anymore. Am I going mad? Or am I finally seeing clearly for the first time?

This boat... the Harbinger... it's more than just a vessel. It's become a purgatory of sorts. A place where I'm forced to confront every mistake, every regret, every person I've wronged.

I don't know how much longer I can endure this. The ghosts, the memories, the guilt... it's all becoming too much. I need to find a way out, but I don't know how. I don't even know if I deserve to escape this.

God help me.

Thirteen

The next morning, Pete stood at the railing of the Harbinger, his hands gripping the cool metal. He hadn't slept all night. He'd lost track of how long he'd been out here, adrift in this watery purgatory.

The sun composed a stunning dawn horizon that should've been beautiful, but to him, it was just another reminder of how far from home he was.

That's when he heard it. Faint at first.

"Pete…"

He blinked, unsure if he'd imagined it. The voice was soft, feminine, almost melodic.

"Pete…"

There it was again, louder this time. He leaned over the railing, peering into the depths below. The water was dark, impenetrable. Yet he could've sworn he saw something move just beneath the surface.

"Who's there?" he called out.

"Pete… come to me…"

The voice was clearer now, unmistakable. There was an otherworldly quality to it, a siren-like allure that both frightened and enticed him.

He shook his head, trying to clear it. This couldn't be real. It was just another hallucination, like the ghostly dinner party or the ever-present albatross. But God, it sounded so real.

THIRTEEN

"Please... help me...," the voice said.

The plea tugged at something deep within him. Despite his better judgment, he found himself leaning further over the railing, straining to catch a glimpse of the voice's owner.

"Where are you?" he called out, desperation creeping into his tone. "I can't see you!"

"Down here... in the water..."

His eyes widened as he saw a pale hand break the surface, reaching up towards him. Without thinking, he stretched out his own hand, fingers grasping at the air.

"I'm coming!" he shouted, already moving to climb over the railing.

But as he swung one leg over, a small part of his mind screamed at him to stop.

He hesitated, his body half over the railing. The voice called again, more insistent this time.

"Pete... please... I need you..."

He closed his eyes, trying to think rationally. But it was so hard. The voice promised an end to his loneliness, a chance at redemption. Maybe if he saved this woman, he could make up for all his past mistakes.

"I... I can't," he finally said, forcing himself to pull back onto the deck. "You're not real. None of this is real."

He stumbled backward, pressing his hands against his ears. But it didn't help. The voice seemed to come from inside his own head now.

"Stop it!" he screamed, falling to his knees on the deck. "Please, just stop!"

His knees ached against the hard deck as he tried to block out the haunting voice. But as it continued to call his name, a sickening realization washed over him. The melodic tone, the slight lilt at the end of each word - it was unmistakable. The voice sounded just like Amy.

"Christ," he muttered, running a hand through his disheveled hair.

"Pete… please…" the voice called, sounding so much like Amy that it made his chest ache.

He thought of the last time he'd seen her, just before this ill-fated trip. The way she'd looked at him with those bright green eyes, full of hope and longing. "When are you going to leave her, Pete?" she'd asked, her fingers tracing patterns on his chest. "You promised."

He'd made a lot of promises. To Amy. To Jennifer. To himself. He'd broken most of them.

The guilt hit him, making him double over on the deck. He thought of Jennifer, practical and steady Jennifer, who'd stood by him through everything. Who'd supported his career, his hobbies, his dreams. And how had he repaid her? With lies and betrayal.

"I'm sorry," he whispered, though he wasn't sure who he was apologizing to. Jennifer? Amy? Or maybe to himself, for the mess he'd made of everything.

The voice called again, more insistent now.

"Pete… I need you…"

He squeezed his eyes shut, trying to block it out. But with his eyes closed, all he could see was Amy's face, hurt and confused, the last time he'd told her he couldn't leave Jennifer. Not yet. He needed more time.

And now here he was, lost at sea, haunted by the ghosts of his mistakes.

He opened his eyes, half-expecting to see Amy's face in the water. But there was nothing there. Just the endless sea.

He pushed himself to his feet, legs shaky beneath him. The voice had stopped, but the memories it had triggered lingered, heavy as an anchor around his neck.

He stumbled to the cabin, collapsing into the chair by his makeshift desk. Once again, he pulled out his journal.

The voice didn't call again, but he could still hear it echoing in his mind.

THIRTEEN

Outside, the sun had fully risen, casting a harsh light over the deck. He squinted against the glare, feeling more lost than ever.

* * *

I heard a voice. God help me, I heard a voice calling my name from the water. It sounded like Amy, but that's impossible. Amy's back in Frederiksted. She can't be here. None of this makes any godamm sense.

Or maybe... Christ, I don't know.

Could it be some kind of siren? I remember reading about them in those old Greek myths. Beautiful women who lured sailors to their deaths with their songs. Is that what's happening to me?

But why would it sound like Amy? Why not Jennifer? She's my wife, for Christ's sake. Shouldn't a siren use her voice if it wanted to lure me? Or maybe that's the point. Maybe it knows about Amy, about...

Maybe it's using my guilt against me.

I keep thinking about all those stories my grandfather used to tell me about the sea. How it could drive a man mad if he spent too long alone on it. How it could play tricks on your mind. I always thought they were just stories, meant to scare kids away from the water. But now...

What if the voice comes back? What if next time, I can't resist it? What if I jump overboard, chasing after a ghost, a memory, a lie?

I don't know what's real anymore. The ghosts on the deck, the voice in the water, the albatross. It's all blending together, and I can't tell where reality ends and my imagination begins.

Maybe that's what the siren wants. To confuse me, to wear me down until I can't fight anymore. Until I give in and let the sea take me.

But I can't. I won't. I have to get back. I have to make things right. With Jennifer. With Amy. With myself.

If I survive this, if I make it back to land, I swear I'll fix everything. I'll be better. I'll—

He stopped writing abruptly, realizing the hypocrisy of his words. How many times had he made similar promises to himself? How many times had he sworn he'd change, only to fall back into the same patterns?

Fourteen

Pete returned to the railing at the edge of the Harbinger where he'd heard the voice before. He stared into the inky blackness of the sea, his eyes straining to make sense of the shadows that danced on the water's surface. The waves against the hull of the Harbinger had once been soothing, but now it felt like a sinister whisper, promising secrets he wasn't sure he wanted to hear.

A flash of iridescent scales caught his eye. But there it was - a face, pale and beautiful, emerging from the depths. His heart nearly stopped as he recognized Jennifer's features, her eyes wide and beseeching.

"Jenny? What the *fuck*?" he said.

As if in response, more faces appeared, surrounding the boat. Some wore Jennifer's visage, others Amy's, their expressions shifting between longing and accusation. He gripped the railing for support as he tried not to collapse.

The faces began to sing, a haunting melody that seemed to vibrate through his very bones. It was a wordless tune, filled with sorrow and desire, almost like an opera, pulling at something deep within him. He found himself leaning forward, drawn by the music and the familiar faces.

As the song wove its spell, memories bubbled to the surface of his mind. He saw himself arguing with Jennifer, her face twisted with hurt and betrayal as she confronted him about Amy. The shame of that moment washed over him anew, making him want to turn away from the apparitions in the water.

But the song wouldn't let him. It shifted, and he was reliving his first encounter with Amy. Her laughter, her spontaneity, the way she made him feel young and alive again. The guilt of those stolen moments mingled with the undeniable thrill, leaving him feeling dizzy and confused.

The *mermaids* - for what else could they be? - circled the boat, their song growing more insistent. He glanced up and noticed the albatross still circling as well, matching the movement of the mermaids. His grip on reality began to slip as more memories surfaced, each one more vivid than the last.

He saw his father's disapproving scowl as he announced his decision to become a psychiatrist instead of following in the family business. The disappointment in those eyes had haunted Pete for years, driving him to prove himself over and over again.

The melody swelled, and Pete found himself reliving a moment he'd buried deep: the day he'd nearly walked away from his practice, overwhelmed by the weight of his patients' troubles. He'd stood on the edge of the pier, staring into the water, wondering if it wouldn't be easier to just let go. It was Jennifer who'd found him there, who'd talked him back from that edge with her quiet strength and unwavering support.

Tears streamed down his face as the weight of his choices crashed over him. The mermaids' song seemed to strip away all his defenses, leaving him raw and exposed. He saw himself as he truly was - not the successful doctor, not the charming lover, but a man running from his own demons, hurting those closest to him in the process.

"I'm sorry," he choked out, not sure if he was addressing the phantoms in the water or the ghosts of his past. "I'm so damn sorry."

The mermaids' faces shifted again, their expressions softening. For a moment, he thought he saw understanding in their eyes, maybe even forgiveness. The song gentled, becoming almost comforting.

The mermaids' melody wrapped around him like a blanket, and for the first time in days, he felt a strange sense of peace. As if by confronting these suppressed truths, he'd taken the first step towards something like redemption.

As the song began to fade, he looked up to find the mermaids sinking back into the depths. Their faces - Jenny's, Amy's, and others he couldn't quite place - gazed at him one last time before disappearing beneath the waves.

Long after the last notes had died away, he remained, staring at the now-still water. He felt hollowed out, but also strangely lighter, as if some of the weight he'd been carrying had been lifted.

Pete stared at the dark water, his body swaying with the gentle rocking of the Harbinger. The mermaids were gone, but their haunting song still echoed in his mind. He felt drained, empty, yet strangely at peace. For a moment, he allowed himself to believe that maybe, just maybe, he could find a way to make things right.

But then the silence settled in, heavy and oppressive. The weight of his choices, his failures, came crashing back down on him. The water below seemed to call to him, promising an escape from the turmoil in his head.

"It'd be so easy," he muttered, leaning forward. "Just one step."

He imagined the coolness of the water enveloping him, washing away his sins. Would it hurt? Or would it be peaceful, like slipping into a dreamless sleep? His foot inched forward, toes curling over the edge of the deck.

A memory flashed through his mind - Jennifer's face, tear-stained but determined, the day she'd found him on the pier. She'd believed in him then, even when he couldn't believe in himself. And Amy, with her carefree laugh and the way she looked at him like he was something special.

His body trembled with indecision. Part of him longed for the oblivion the sea promised, but another part clung desperately to life, to the possibility of redemption. He closed his eyes, feeling the spray of the ocean on his face.

"I'm sorry," he whispered again, though he wasn't sure who he was apologizing to anymore.

His muscles tensed, ready to push off from the deck. But something held him back - fear, hope, or maybe just stubborn pride. He opened his eyes, staring down at the waves below.

"Not like this," he said through gritted teeth. "Not fucking like this."

With a herculean effort, he forced himself to take a step back from the railing. His legs felt like jelly, and he collapsed onto the deck. He lay there for a long time, listening to the sound of the waves against the hull and the distant cry of the albatross overhead.

* * *

My dearest ladies of the deep,

I can't get your voices out of my head. They echo in my dreams, in the spaces between thoughts. Christ, I must be losing it, writing to mermaids. But who else is there to talk to out here?

You called to me, and I almost answered. I wanted to. Maybe I should have. You're probably the only ones who'd understand me now. Everyone else - Jennifer, Amy, my old man - they're all so far away. But you, you're right here, just beneath the waves.

I saw your faces, you know. Sometimes you looked like Jennifer, sometimes

FOURTEEN

like Amy. Is that what you do? Show a man what he wants to see? Or is it what he fears? Hell if I know anymore.

Your song, it was beautiful. Sad, though. Made me think of all the things I've screwed up. All the people I've hurt. You get that, don't you? The loneliness, the ache of it all. That's why you sing, isn't it?

I wonder what it's like down there, in your world. Quiet, maybe. Peaceful. No expectations, no disappointments. Just the endless blue. Sometimes I think I can hear you calling me still, whispering my name on the wind.

Do you ever get lonely down there? Or are there too many of you to ever feel alone? I bet you understand each other, at least. Not like up here, where everything's a godamm mess of misunderstandings and hurt feelings.

I keep thinking about your eyes. They were so deep, so full of... something. Understanding? Pity? I don't know. But for a moment there, I felt seen. Really seen, you know? Not the successful Dr. Corbin, not the cheating husband, not the disappointment of a son. Just... me. Pete. Whoever the hell that is anymore.

Maybe that's why I'm writing this. To try and hold onto that feeling. To pretend, for a little while, that someone out there gets it. Gets me.

Jesus, listen to me. Pouring my heart out to imaginary fish-women. If my patients could see me now, huh? Some psychiatrist I turned out to be. Can't even keep my own head straight.

But you don't judge, do you? You just sing your song and wait. Patient. Eternal. Maybe that's what I need. Just to let go of all this... bullshit. All the expectations and the guilt and the fear.

I keep thinking about what it would be like to join you. To slip beneath the waves and leave all this behind. Would you welcome me? Or am I too tainted, too human?

Ah, hell. What am I even saying? You're not real. None of this is real. I'm just a lonely, fucked-up man on a boat, talking to himself. When did the nuts take over the nut-house, anyway?

But if you are out there, if you can hear me somehow... thank you. For the *song. For the moment of peace. For making me feel, just for a second, like I wasn't alone out here.*

Maybe I'll hear you again tonight. Maybe this time, I'll be brave enough to answer.

Until then, my beautiful, impossible friends,
Pete

He closed the journal and looked out at the water, half-hoping, half-fearing to see a flash of scales or hear a distant melody.

Fifteen

Pete squinted, his eyes scanning the horizon. He was about to turn away when something caught his eye.

At first, he thought it was a trick of the light. But there, in the distance, a massive shape breached the surface of the water.

"Holy shit," he muttered, fumbling for his binoculars.

Through the lenses, he could make out the unmistakable form of a sperm whale. A *white*... sperm whale. It was enormous, its albino skin gleaming in the sunlight. As it surfaced, a plume of mist erupted from its blowhole, hanging in the air like a spectral banner.

He lowered the binoculars, his hands shaking. He'd seen whales before, sure, but never like this. Never this close, and never one so... *white*.

"Moby Dick," he whispered, then laughed at his own absurdity. "Godamm Moby fucking Dick. Christ, Corbin, get a grip."

But the comparison lingered in his mind as he watched the whale. It moved with a grace that belied its massive size, cutting through the water like a living submarine. Every now and then, its flukes would break the surface, sending up a spray that caught the light like diamonds.

He found himself transfixed. There was something mesmerizing about the creature, something almost... purposeful. As if it knew he was watching. As if it had come here, to this exact spot in the endless ocean, just for him.

"That's crazy talk," he muttered, but he couldn't shake the feeling.

The whale dove, disappearing beneath the waves. Pete held his breath, counting the seconds. One minute passed. Then two. Just as he was beginning to think it was gone for good, it resurfaced, closer this time.

He could see its eye now, a dark, intelligent orb that seemed to stare right through him. He felt exposed, laid bare before this ancient creature of the deep. All his sins, all his failures - the affairs, the lies, the disappointments - they all seemed to shrink in the face of this timeless leviathan.

"What do you want?" he found himself asking aloud. "Why are you here?"

The whale just continued its slow, majestic circuit around the boat. Pete tracked its movement, feeling a mix of awe and unease. There was something almost biblical about the scene, like he was witnessing some kind of divine judgment.

As the whale passed close to the boat, he could see scars crisscrossing its white hide. Old wounds, testament to battles fought in the depths. He thought of his own scars, the invisible ones that had driven him out here in the first place.

"We're not so different, you and I," he said softly. "Both of us, alone out here, carrying our history on our skin."

The whale breached then, its massive body arcing out of the water in a spectacular display of power. Pete stumbled back, nearly falling as the boat rocked in the resulting waves. Water rained down, soaking him to the skin, but he hardly noticed.

All he could see was the whale, hanging there for a moment in defiance of gravity, before crashing back into the sea with a thunderous splash. The sound echoed across the water, seeming to shake the very air.

He stood there, dripping and stunned, his heart pounding. He

FIFTEEN

felt changed somehow, as if that display had shifted something fundamental inside him. The whale surfaced again, closer than ever, its eye once more finding Pete's.

In that moment, he felt a connection, an understanding that transcended words. He saw in that ancient gaze a reflection of his own loneliness, his own struggles. But he also saw something else - a strength, a resilience that had allowed this creature to survive countless years in the unforgiving sea.

As the whale began to move away, he felt a sudden, irrational urge to follow it. To leave behind the boat, his last tether to the world he knew, and plunge into the unknown depths. For a wild moment, he almost did it. Just like he almost had with the mermaids.

But then the spell broke. The whale dove again, its flukes lifting high in a salute before disappearing beneath the waves. He watched the spot where it had vanished. The sea was once again quiet, as if the whole encounter had been nothing more than another hallucination.

Yet he knew it had been real. He could still feel the spray on his skin, could still see the intelligence in that dark eye. Whatever else might be going on in his fractured psyche, this, at least, had happened.

* * *

Pete had been pacing the deck for an hour, his mind still buzzing from the encounter with the white whale. He couldn't shake the feeling that something profound had occurred, something that went beyond the realm of the ordinary. The memory of those intelligent eyes, that scarred white hide, kept replaying in his mind.

He was so lost in thought that he almost missed it at first - a disturbance in the water, far off on the horizon. He blinked, rubbing his eyes. When he looked again, his breath caught in his throat.

The whale was back.

He felt his heart begin to race as he watched the creature approach. With each passing moment, it seemed to grow larger, its proportions swelling to monstrous sizes. This wasn't the majestic, awe-inspiring creature he'd seen before. This was something else entirely.

"Jesus Christ," he shouted, stumbling backward as the whale drew nearer. Its eye alone was now the size of his boat, a dark abyss that seemed to swallow all light. The scars on its hide had transformed into deep, angry gouges that oozed a dark substance into the churning water.

The whale's movements were different too. Gone was the graceful glide through the water. Now, it thrashed and churned, sending up massive waves that threatened to capsize the boat. Pete clung to the railing, his knuckles turned white with the effort of keeping himself upright.

"This is unreal," he told himself, even as he felt the spray from the whale's violent movements soak through his clothes.

But real or not, the whale was coming straight for him. Its massive jaws opened, revealing row upon row of teeth, each one as long as Pete's arm. The sound that emerged was like nothing he had ever heard before - a deep, resonant bellow that seemed to vibrate the very air around him.

He scrambled for the wheel, his hands shaking as he tried to start the engine. It sputtered once, twice, before roaring to life. He yanked the wheel hard, turning the boat away from the oncoming behemoth.

But the whale was faster. It dove beneath the surface, only to emerge moments later right beside the boat. The impact sent Pete sprawling across the deck. He could hear the wood creaking and groaning under the strain.

As he struggled to his feet, he found himself face to face with the

FIFTEEN

whale's enormous eye. In its depths, he saw not the wisdom and understanding of before, but something darker. Something hungry.

"What do you want?" he screamed, his voice lost in the chaos of churning water and creaking wood. "Why are you doing this?"

The whale's only response was another earth-shattering bellow. It began to circle the boat, each pass bringing it closer. Pete could see every detail of its monstrous form now - the barnacles clinging to its hide, the scars that seemed to pulse with an otherworldly light.

With each circle, the whale's size seemed to increase. Soon, it dwarfed not just the Harbinger, but any whale that had ever existed. Its body stretched across the horizon, blotting out the sun and casting Pete's world into shadow.

He felt something snap inside him. This was beyond fear, beyond terror. He began to laugh, a high, hysterical sound that bubbled up from somewhere deep inside him. Here he was, Dr. Pete Corbin, successful psychiatrist, adulterer, liar - about to be swallowed whole by a whale straight out of Hell, itself.

The whale made one final pass, its eye fixed on Pete. Then, with a motion that seemed to split the very ocean, it opened its massive jaws and lunged.

Pete closed his eyes, bracing for the end. He could feel the hot breath of the creature, smell the ancient, briny scent of its gullet. This was it. This was how it ended.

But the end didn't come. Instead, he felt a sudden, violent lurch. His eyes flew open just in time to see the whale's massive form pass overhead, missing the boat by mere inches. The displacement of water sent the boat rocking wildly, nearly capsizing it.

As he clung to the railing, gasping for breath, he watched the whale continue its charge, its unbelievable bulk stretching as far as the eye could see. Then, slowly, it began to shrink, its form receding into the distance until it was nothing more than a speck on the horizon.

And then, just like that, it was gone again.

He stood there, soaked to the bone and shaking, staring at the now-calm sea. The only evidence of what had just occurred was the rocking of the Harbinger and the racing of his heart.

"What the hell," he whispered, his voice hoarse. "What the hell was that?"

Pete stood on the deck of the Harbinger. As the initial shock began to wear off, a strange determination took its place.

"No," he muttered, clenching his fists. "I'm not going to be some helpless victim. If that thing comes back, I'll be ready."

With a newfound sense of purpose, he began to scour the boat for anything he could use as a weapon. He ransacked the cabin, tearing through drawers and cabinets. He pulled out a large fishing knife, its blade glinting in the dim light.

"It's not a harpoon, but it'll have to do," he said, gripping the handle tightly.

His mind spun with half-remembered scenes from Moby Dick, a book he'd read years ago. He'd always thought of himself as more of an Ishmael than an Ahab, but now, faced with this insane situation, he felt a kinship with the obsessed captain he'd never understood before.

He stumbled back onto the deck, knife in hand, and began to lash it to the end of a fishing rod. The makeshift harpoon was crude, but it gave him a sense of control he desperately needed.

"Come on, you bastard," he growled, scanning the horizon. "Come back and face me."

As if in response to his challenge, a dark shape appeared in the distance. His breath caught in his throat as he watched it grow larger, approaching with incredible speed.

"Steady," he told himself, gripping his homemade weapon. "Steady now."

FIFTEEN

The whale breached the surface with a thunderous splash, water cascading off its scarred white hide. Its eye, black as night and large as the moon, fixed on Pete with what he could only describe as malevolent intelligence.

Pete raised his makeshift harpoon, aiming it at the massive creature.

"From hell's heart, I stab at thee," he shouted, the words coming unexpectedly to his lips, channeling his inner Captain Ahab.

The whale let out a bellow that shook the very air, and charged. Pete stood his ground, his arms trembling but his aim true. As the behemoth drew near, he hurled his weapon with all his might.

The harpoon sailed through the air, a pitiful thing against the whale's massive bulk. It struck the creature's hide and bounced off harmlessly, lost to the churning sea.

Pete stared in disbelief, his last hope disappearing beneath the waves. The whale's charge didn't slow, its massive form bearing down on the Harbinger with unstoppable force.

"Oh, God," he said, stumbling backward. "Oh, God, no."

The impact, when it came, was like nothing he had ever experienced. The boat lurched violently, throwing him off his feet. He hit the deck hard, the breath knocked from his lungs.

As he struggled to rise, he saw the whale circling back for another pass. Its eye found him again, and in that moment, he understood. This wasn't just some animal. This was something else entirely, something beyond his comprehension.

He scrambled to his feet, his mind racing. What would Ahab do? What would any of them do in the face of this unstoppable foe?

Sixteen

The Harbinger rocked violently, the whale's massive body slamming against the hull. The sound of splintering wood filled the air, and Pete felt the deck shift beneath his feet. "Jesus Christ," he shouted.

The whale circled back. He scrambled across the deck, searching for anything he could use as another weapon. His hand closed around a loose piece of railing, torn free in the initial impact.

As the whale charged again, he swung the makeshift club wildly.

"Come on, you son of a bitch!" he shouted, his voice cracking.

The impact sent shockwaves through the boat. He lost his footing and tumbled across the deck, slamming into the cabin wall. Pain shot through his shoulder, and he tasted blood in his mouth.

He struggled to his feet, dizzy and disoriented. The Harbinger listed to one side, taking on water. He staggered to the edge and peered over, seeing a gaping hole in the hull where the whale had struck.

"No, no, no," he said, panic rising in his chest. He rushed to the cabin, searching for the emergency repair kit he knew was stored somewhere.

The boat lurched again as the whale struck from below. Pete was thrown against the cabin door, his head connecting with the frame. Stars exploded in his vision, and for a moment, he thought he might pass out.

He shook his head, trying to clear it.

SIXTEEN

"Focus, damn it," he told himself. "You've got to focus."

He found the repair kit and stumbled back onto the deck. The whale was circling again, its massive form visible just beneath the surface. He dropped to his knees by the damaged section of hull, fumbling with the kit's contents.

As he worked to patch the hole, his mind raced. This couldn't be real. Whales didn't behave like this. They didn't target boats, didn't attack with such relentless fury. But the pain in his body, the terror in his heart – those felt all too real.

The whale breached again, this time on the opposite side of the boat. Water cascaded over the deck, soaking Pete to the bone. He watched in horror as the creature's massive tail came down on the bow of the Harbinger.

The impact was devastating. The entire front of the boat crumpled like it was made of paper. Pete was thrown backward, skidding across the wet deck. He came to a stop against the cabin, the wind knocked out of him.

For a moment, he lay there, gasping for breath. The Harbinger groaned and creaked around him, the sounds of a dying vessel. He forced himself to his feet, his body screaming in protest.

The boat was taking on water fast now. The bow was almost entirely submerged, and the stern was lifting out of the water. He stumbled to the radio, praying it still worked.

"Mayday, mayday," he shouted into the receiver. "This is the Harbinger. We're under attack. I need immediate assistance!"

Only static answered him. He slammed the radio down in frustration. He turned back to the deck, searching for any sign of the whale.

The sea was calm now, almost eerily so. His eyes darted from wave to wave, expecting to see that massive white form at any moment. But there was nothing.

A loud crack echoed across the water, and he felt the Harbinger shudder beneath him. He looked down to see a fissure spreading across the deck, the boat literally breaking apart.

"No," he said, his voice barely a whisper. "This can't be happening."

He made a desperate dash for the life raft. As he ran, he could hear the boat groaning and splitting behind him.

Just as he was about to reach it, a shadow fell over him. He looked up to see the whale, impossibly huge, rising out of the water beside the boat. Its eye, black and fathomless, seemed to stare right into his soul.

Pete stood frozen. The whale opened its massive jaws, revealing rows of massive teeth. And then, instead of delivering the final death blow… it was gone.

Pete stared at the calm sea, his heart still racing from the encounter with the whale. The Harbinger bobbed gently on the waves, damaged, but miraculously intact. Nothing like the damage he had perceived earlier. He blinked, trying to make sense of it.

"What the hell?" he muttered, running a hand through his salt-crusted hair.

As the adrenaline began to fade, he became aware of a sharp pain in his left arm. He looked down, expecting to see nothing more than a bruise from his tumble across the deck. Instead, he found a deep gash running from his elbow to his wrist, blood oozing slowly from the wound.

"Damn," he hissed, cradling his arm.

He stumbled to the cabin, his legs shaky beneath him. He rummaged through the first aid kit, pulling out gauze and antiseptic. As he cleaned the wound, he tried to piece together the events of the past hour. The whale, the destruction of the boat, the desperate fight for survival - it had all felt so real. But here he was, on a *mostly* undamaged boat with nothing but a cut on his arm to show for it.

He wrapped the gauze around his arm, wincing at the pressure. Once

SIXTEEN

finished, he leaned back against the cabin wall, closing his eyes. The exhaustion of the imaginary battle weighed heavily on him.

When he opened his eyes again, the sun had shifted in the sky. He must have dozed off. He glanced at his arm, ready to change the bandage, but froze. The gauze was gone. So was the cut.

"What the fuck?"

He examined his arm, turning it over in the light. The skin was unmarked, not even a scar to show where the gash had been.

He distinctly remembered the pain, the blood, the act of bandaging the wound. How could it just disappear?

As if in answer to his unspoken question, a sharp pain flared in his right leg. He rolled up his pant leg, revealing a deep purple bruise on his calf that hadn't been there before. He pressed it gently, wincing at the tenderness.

"This isn't possible," he said, his voice shaky.

He limped to the deck, scanning the horizon. The expanse of water offered no explanations, no comfort. He was alone with his increasingly unreliable perceptions.

The bruise on his leg throbbed, a constant reminder of his confusion. He sat down heavily on the deck. Was this some sort of hallucination brought on by dehydration or exposure?

He closed his eyes, took a deep breath, and counted to ten. When he opened them, he half-expected the bruise to be gone. Instead, he found a series of small cuts across the back of his hand, as if he'd run it through broken glass.

"No," he said, shaking his head.

He blinked hard, willing the cuts to disappear. When he looked again, they were gone - replaced by a burn mark on his forearm.

He scrambled to his feet, panic rising in his chest. He rushed to the small mirror in the cabin, examining his reflection. As he watched, a black eye bloomed and faded, replaced by a split lip that sealed itself in seconds.

"This isn't real," he said to his reflection.

But the pain felt real. Each injury, no matter how briefly it existed, brought with it a sharp, undeniable sensation. He found himself actually *longing* for the simplicity of the whale attack. At least then, he understood what was happening, even if it was a delusion. Or was it? What had damaged the boat? Even though it was considerably less than he'd imagined.

He stumbled back to the deck. The injuries continued to appear and disappear, each one adding to his confusion. A sprained wrist. A twisted ankle. A dislocated shoulder that popped back into place as quickly as it had appeared.

His reality had become a kaleidoscope of pain and healing, each sensation blurring into the next. The line between his physical experience and his mental state had blurred beyond recognition.

As he stood there, trying to make sense of his shifting reality, he realized that the true injury wasn't to his body, but to his grip on reality itself. And that, he feared, might be a wound that wouldn't heal so easily.

* * *

Call me Pete. Some time ago—never mind how long precisely—having little or no money in my purse, and nothing particular to interest me on shore, I thought I would sail about a little and see the watery part of the world. It is a way I have of driving off the spleen and regulating the circulation.

He paused, frowning at the words he'd just written. They weren't his own, not entirely, yet they felt right. He continued:

SIXTEEN

But lo, what seemed a simple voyage has become a quest of vengeance, a battle against a foe as vast and inscrutable as the sea itself. For I have seen the white whale, that pasteboard mask of malice, that wall of inscrutable whiteness thrust before me.

Like Ahab before me, I find myself locked in combat with a creature beyond mortal ken. The Harbinger, my faithful vessel, creaks and groans beneath me, bearing the scars of our encounter. Yet when I look upon her timbers, I see naught but phantom wounds, injuries that appear and vanish like mirages on the horizon.

And what of my own flesh? It, too, bears the marks of our battle, only to heal and be rent anew in an endless cycle of torment. Am I, like the fabled Prometheus, doomed to suffer eternally for my hubris? Or is this some trick of the mind, a fever dream brought on by too long at sea?

I cannot say with certainty whether the whale I faced was real or imagined. Perhaps it matters not. For in this vastness of blue, where the line between sky and sea blurs into infinity, what is real and what is dream become one and the same.

I find myself pondering the nature of my quest. What white whale do I truly pursue? Is it redemption I seek, or merely escape from the life I've left behind? The faces of those I've wronged haunt me more surely than any spectral leviathan.

My dear Jennifer, my Amy—are they not like Ahab's wife, left behind while I chase my own destruction across the endless waves? And my father, stern Jonathon, is he not like the implacable God that Ahab railed against?

Yet I cannot turn back. Like Ahab, I am bound to this course, compelled by forces I scarcely understand. The albatross circles overhead, a constant reminder of my folly. Is it a harbinger of doom, or merely a witness to my descent into madness?

The sea whispers its secrets, but I lack the wisdom to decipher them. I am adrift, not just upon the waters, but within my own mind. Reality shifts and changes like the tides, leaving me unmoored and uncertain.

But I shall persevere. For what is man if not a creature of will, set against the indifference of the universe? I shall face my white whale, be it beast or demon or my own tormented psyche.

And if I am to meet my end in this pursuit, let it be said that I went willingly into that final embrace. For in the end, are we not all bound for the depths, to sleep with the leviathans in the quiet darkness of the ocean floor?

Call me Pete. Call me Ahab. Call me a fool chasing shadows across the endless sea. Whatever name you give me, know that I sail on, into the heart of my own personal maelstrom, seeking answers to questions I dare not voice aloud.

The whale awaits. The chase continues. And I, Pete Corbin, am both hunter and hunted on this massive, unforgiving, hellscape of a sea.

Pete's words seemed to blend before him, blurring the line between his own thoughts and the echoes of Melville's prose. He wasn't sure where the story ended and his reality began anymore. But then again, did it really matter?

Seventeen

Pete stood and surveyed the damage to the Harbinger with confusion, but determination. The battle with the whale—real or imagined—had *somehow* left its mark on his vessel. He ran his hand along the splintered edge, feeling the roughness beneath his fingers.

"Gotta fix this," he muttered to himself. He made his way to the storage compartment, rummaging through tools and supplies. The familiar weight of a hammer in his hand brought a fleeting sense of normalcy.

He set to work, replacing the broken sections. The repetitive motion of hammering nails into wood helped clear his mind, if only temporarily. Sweat beaded on his forehead as he worked under the relentless sun.

As he moved along the deck, he noticed other areas of damage. A crack ran along the port side, water seeping in slowly but steadily. He frowned, realizing this would require more extensive repairs.

He retrieved a bucket and began to bail out the water that had accumulated in the bottom of the boat. The physical exertion felt good, grounding him in reality. Or what he hoped was reality.

"This is real," he said aloud, his own voice startling him against the empty silence of the sea. "This damage is real. I can fix this."

He found some sealant in the supplies and began to patch the crack.

As he worked, he couldn't shake the nagging doubt in the back of his mind. Hadn't he seen these damages appear and disappear before? Were his efforts futile against the shifting nature of his perception?

He shook his head, trying to dispel these thoughts. He focused on the task at hand, meticulously applying the sealant. The smell of the chemicals was sharp and acrid, cutting through the salty air.

As he finished sealing the crack, he noticed something odd. The damage seemed to extend further than he initially thought. He followed the line of the crack, finding it snaked across the deck.

"No," he muttered, his heart rate increasing.

He squeezed his eyes shut, trying to clear his vision. When he opened them, the extended crack was gone. Only the section he had just repaired remained.

He sat back on his heels. The repairs were real. He could feel the texture of the sealant, smell its pungent odor. This was tangible, concrete.

He stood up, deciding to check the rest of the boat for damage. As he moved around, he found more areas that needed attention. A loose board here, a bent railing there. Each repair felt like a small victory against the chaos that threatened to overwhelm him.

As he worked, he couldn't help but draw parallels to his life on land. Wasn't this what he had always done? Patching up the cracks, fixing the surface damage, all while ignoring the deeper issues that threatened to sink him?

He paused in his work, looking out at the water surrounding him. The albatross was above as always. Did it never need to eat? Was it even really there at all? He wasn't sure anymore.

With a sigh, he returned to his repairs. The physical labor was therapeutic, giving him a sense of purpose. For a moment, he could pretend he was just a man on a boat, fixing what was broken. Not a lost soul adrift in a sea of confusion and guilt.

SEVENTEEN

As the sun began to set, he surveyed his work. The boat looked better, sturdier. But he couldn't shake the feeling that it was all temporary, that the damage would return, shifting and changing like everything else in this surreal journey.

He leaned against the repaired railing, feeling it beneath his hands. For now, at least, this was real. This, he could hold onto.

Then, he heard it. A loud cracking sound.

* * *

Pete stared in disbelief at the new damages that had appeared on the Harbinger. Cracks spider-webbed across the deck, and the hull groaned ominously. The repairs he'd just made seemed to mock him, islands of stability in a sea of destruction.

"Shit," he said,. "This can't be happening."

But it was. The boat was falling apart around him, and no amount of patching would save it now. He frantically searched for a solution. He couldn't stay on his beloved Harbinger—she was doomed. But he couldn't just jump into the ocean either.

A raft. He needed to build a raft. Unfortunately, the Harbinger's life raft's were all lost during the *imaginary* battle with Moby Dick's twin.

He scrambled to gather materials. He tore off pieces of the railing, ignoring the splinters that dug into his palms. He yanked up loose floorboards, his muscles straining with the effort. Every creak and groan of the boat spurred him to move faster.

He found some rope in the storage compartment and began lashing the pieces together. His hands shook as he worked, making the knots clumsy and loose. He cursed, undid them, and started again.

"Come on, come on," he muttered.

The albatross hovered overhead, its cry seeming to laugh at him.

He glanced up at the bird, his eyes narrowing.

"You think this is funny, don't you? Well, screw you. I'm getting off this damn boat."

He returned to his work with renewed vigor. The raft began to take shape, a crude assembly of wood and hope. He added anything he could find that might float—empty barrels, life preservers.

As he worked, his mind wandered. He thought of Jennifer, of the argument they'd had before he left. He thought of Amy, and the guilt that gnawed at him. He thought of his father, and wondered what the old man would say if he could see him now.

Probably tell me I'm doing it all wrong, he thought, a bitter laugh escaping his lips.

Sweat stung his eyes and his muscles ached, but he didn't stop. He couldn't stop. The Harbinger creaked and shifted beneath him, reminding him of the urgency of his task.

Finally, after what felt like hours, he stepped back to survey his work. The raft was ugly and misshapen, but it looked like it might float. It had to float. He had no other choice.

He began to gather supplies for the raft. Food, water, his journal—anything he thought might help him survive. As he moved around the boat, he noticed more damage appearing. A new crack here, a widening hole there. The Harbinger was falling apart faster than he could comprehend.

"Just hold on a little longer," he pleaded with the boat, as if it could hear him. "Just a little longer."

He returned to the raft, securing the supplies as best he could.

"You want to see me fail, don't you?" he shouted at the albatross. "Well, I won't. You hear me? I won't!"

Pete's outburst was met with silence, broken only by the creaking of the boat and the crashing of waves against the hull. He needed to focus. The raft was his only chance now.

As he made the final preparations to launch his makeshift vessel, he couldn't help but wonder if this was all futile. Was he really going to set out on this cobbled-together raft, in the middle of the ocean? Was this any better than staying on the sinking Harbinger?

But what choice did he have? The boat was falling apart around him. He had to try something, anything, to survive.

He looked at the raft, then back at the Harbinger. The boat that had been his escape, his sanctuary, was now a deathtrap. He felt a pang of sadness, mixed with a strange sense of relief. Maybe leaving the Harbinger behind meant leaving behind all the baggage he'd brought with him—the guilt, the regret, the fear.

"Okay," he said. "Okay. Let's do this."

He began to push the raft towards the edge of the boat, ready to launch it into the water. The Harbinger groaned beneath him, as if protesting his departure. He gritted his teeth and pushed harder, determined to see this through.

As Pete strained to push the raft towards the edge of the boat, he felt a sudden warmth beside him. He turned his head, and there she was—Amy, her blonde hair whipping in the wind, her green eyes fixed on him with that familiar intensity.

"Need a hand, sailor?" she asked, a wry smile playing on her lips.

She couldn't be here. It wasn't possible. And yet...

"Amy?" he croaked. "What are you—how did you—"

She laughed, the sound carrying over the creaking of the Harbinger.

"Always so many questions with you, Pete. Can't you just be glad to see me?"

He shook his head.

"You're not real."

Amy shrugged, placing her hands on the raft.

"Real or not, looks like you could use some help. Come on, push with me."

Despite his confusion, he found himself working alongside her, their bodies moving in sync as they pushed the raft closer to the edge.

"Remember when we first met?" Amy asked, her voice light despite the effort.

He nodded, memories flooding back.

"You were such a gentleman," Amy said. "That's when I knew you were different."

They pushed in silence for a moment, the only sounds the groaning of the Harbinger and their labored breathing.

"We shouldn't have started this, Amy," he said finally, his voice low. "It was wrong from the beginning."

Amy's face hardened.

"Don't say that. What we had is real, Pete. More real than anything in your life."

"I have a wife," he protested weakly.

"A wife you're running from," Amy shot back. "Why else would you be out here, Pete? Why else would you have asked me to come with you?"

He froze, his hands slipping from the raft.

"What? I never—"

"Oh, but you did," Amy insisted, her eyes flashing. "Don't you remember? The night before you left, you came to me. You said you were leaving for good, that you wanted me to come with you. Start a new life together."

His mind began to burn. Had he really done that? He remembered going to see Amy before he left, but the details were fuzzy. Had he really asked her to run away with him?

"I... I don't remember," he said.

Amy's face softened.

SEVENTEEN

"It's okay, Pete. You were upset that night. Said something about a fight with Jennifer, about how you couldn't take it anymore."

They resumed pushing the raft, but his movements were mechanical now, his mind elsewhere.

"But you... didn't... come," he said slowly. "If I asked you, why didn't you come?"

Amy's laugh was bitter this time.

"Oh, I came alright. I was at the marina that morning, bag packed, ready to start our new life. But you..." She trailed off, shaking her head.

"What?" he pressed. "What happened?"

"You looked right through me," Amy said, her voice barely above a whisper. "Like you didn't even see me. You just got on your boat and sailed away. Left me standing there like a fool."

He felt a wave of guilt wash over him. "Amy, I'm so sorry. I don't—I can't remember—"

"It's fine," she cut him off. "I get it. You were scared. Having second thoughts. But I'm here now, aren't I? We can still have our fresh start. Be together *forever*."

They had reached the edge of the boat now. The raft teetered precariously, ready to be launched into the unforgiving sea.

Eighteen

Pete stared at Amy. The guilt he'd been suppressing bubbled to the surface, threatening to overwhelm him.

"You're not real," he said again, more forcefully this time. "You can't be here."

Amy's eyes flashed with anger.

"I'm as real as you want me to be, Pete. Or are you trying to *erase* me, just like you did that morning?"

"I didn't—I wouldn't—" he stammered, but the words caught in his throat.

"Wouldn't what?" Amy challenged, taking a step towards him. "Wouldn't lead me on? Wouldn't make me fall in love with you? Wouldn't promise me a future you had no intention of delivering?"

He felt his own anger rising to meet hers.

"That's not fair! I never really promised you anything!"

"Bullshit!" Amy spat. "You promised me everything! A new life, away from all this. Away from your wife, your job. You promised me freedom, Pete."

"I was drunk!" he shouted, the words escaping before he could stop them. "That night, before I left. I was drunk, and scared, and... and stupid."

Amy's face contorted with hurt and rage.

"So that's it? It was all just a drunken mistake to you?"

EIGHTEEN

"No! I mean, yes! I mean…" He ran his hands through his hair, frustration building. "I don't know what I mean anymore. This whole thing—us—it was a mistake from the start."

"A mistake?" Amy's voice was dangerously quiet now. "Is that what you tell yourself to sleep at night, Pete? That I'm just some mistake you can *erase*?"

"You don't understand," he said, his voice breaking. "I have a life, responsibilities. I can't just throw it all away."

"Can't? Or won't?" Amy challenged. "Face it, Pete. You're a coward. You're out here running away from everything, including me… and what you *did* to me."

He felt something snap inside him.

"You want to talk about cowardice? Fine. Let's talk about how you knew I was married from the start. How you pursued me anyway. How you never once cared about the consequences, about who might get hurt!"

Amy recoiled as if she'd been slapped.

"Don't you dare put this all on me. You were a willing participant, Pete. More than willing. Or have you conveniently forgotten all those nights we spent together? All those promises you whispered in my ear, in the dark, as you screwed me?"

His guilt surged again, but he pushed it down.

"I never should have let it go that far. I should have ended it before…"

"Before what?" Amy demanded. "Before you fell in love with me?"

"I'm not in love with you!" he shouted, his voice echoing across the water. "I love my wife!"

The moment the words left his mouth, he knew they were a lie. Or at least, not the whole truth. He did love Jennifer, in his way. But Amy… Amy had awakened something in him he thought long dead.

Amy seemed to sense his inner conflict. Her expression softened slightly.

"If you love her so much, why are you out here, Pete? Why did you run away?"

His shoulders slumped.

"I don't know," he admitted. "I thought... I thought I could figure things out. Make sense of everything."

"And have you?" Amy asked, her voice gentler now. "Made sense of anything?"

He looked at her, really looked at her. Even as a hallucination, she was beautiful. Vibrant. Alive in a way that made his heart ache.

"No," he said softly. "I haven't. I'm more lost now than ever."

Amy reached out, her hand hovering just above his cheek. He could almost feel her warmth.

"You don't have to be lost anymore, Pete," she whispered. "I'm here now. We can finally be together."

For a moment, he was tempted. So tempted to give in, to let this fantasy—this hallucination—sweep him away. But reality crashed back in, cold and unforgiving as the sea around them.

"No," he said, taking a step back. "No, we can't. Because you're not real, Amy. You're just... you're just my guilt made manifest. My fears. My regrets."

Amy's face crumpled.

"So that's it? You're just going to push me away... *again*?"

He felt tears stinging his eyes.

"I have to. What we had... it wasn't real. It couldn't be. I'm sorry, Amy. I'm so, so sorry."

As he spoke the words, Amy began to fade, becoming translucent.

"You can't run forever, Pete," she said, her voice growing fainter. "Sooner or later, you'll have to face the truth of what you did."

And then she was gone, leaving him alone on the deck of the Harbinger with his crude raft.

EIGHTEEN

Pete stared at the makeshift... thing... before him, his last hope for salvation, as it crumbled before his eyes. The lashings he'd so carefully tied came undone, planks of wood sliding apart like a poorly constructed jigsaw puzzle. He watched, helpless, as his creation disintegrated into nothing more than flotsam.

"No, godammit," he said, scrambling to grab the pieces before they fell over the edge of the boat and drifted away. His hands, raw and blistered from hours of work, fumbled with the slippery wood. Each plank he managed to snatch felt like a cruel joke—what good was one plank against the the ocean?

"Fuck!" he shouted, kicking at a stubborn piece of wood that refused to budge. Pain shot through his foot, and he hopped awkwardly, nearly losing his balance.

He sank to his knees. He ran his hands over the splintered remains of his raft, feeling each imperfection, each flaw in his design. How could he have been so stupid? So careless? He was a doctor, for Christ's sake. He should have known better than to think he could build a seaworthy vessel from scraps.

The albatross circled overhead, its massive wings casting fleeting shadows across the deck.

"Happy now?" he yelled at the bird. "Is this what you wanted?"

He dragged himself to his feet, swaying slightly as a wave of dizziness washed over him. He stumbled to the railing, gripping it tightly as he surveyed the endless blue stretching out in every direction. No land in sight. No ships. No hope.

He thought about jumping. It would be easy, wouldn't it? Just one step over the railing, and it would all be over. No more guilt, no more fear, no more choices. Just the cool embrace of the sea, pulling him down into its depths.

But something held him back yet again. Maybe it was cowardice. Maybe it was that stubborn will to live that had gotten him this far.

He turned away from the railing, his gaze falling on the scattered remains of his raft. He couldn't give up. Not yet. Not when there was still a chance, however slim, of survival. With a deep breath, he bent down and began gathering the pieces once more.

His muscles screamed in protest as he worked, hauling planks and coils of rope back to the center of the deck.

Hours passed, or maybe it was minutes. Time had lost all meaning out here on the open sea. He worked tirelessly, his movements becoming more frantic, more desperate with each passing moment. He tied knots until his fingers bled, ignoring the pain, focused solely on his task.

But no matter how hard he tried, the raft refused to take shape. Each time he thought he'd made progress, something would slip, or a knot would come undone, and he'd be back where he started. It was like trying to build a house of cards in a hurricane.

Finally, exhausted and defeated, he collapsed onto the deck. He lay there, panting, staring up at the cloudless sky. The albatross wheeled by.

"What do you want from me? I've tried, okay? I've tried to fix this, to make it right. But I can't. I can't fix any of it."

Tears welled up in his eyes, spilling over and mixing with the sweat on his face.

"I'm sorry," he said again, to no one and everyone at once. "I'm so fucking sorry."

The sound of wood scraping against wood drew his attention. He turned his head, watching as the last intact piece of his raft slid across the deck, pushed by a gentle wave. It teetered on the edge for a moment before falling into the sea with a soft splash.

He closed his eyes, listening to the rhythmic ebb and flow of waves.. He was utterly defeated now. The raft had been his last hope, his final attempt at taking control of his fate. And now, like everything else in his life, it had fallen apart.

EIGHTEEN

He lay there, motionless, lost in thought, replaying every mistake, every misstep that had led him to this moment.

He finally pushed himself up, wincing at the stiffness in his muscles. He looked around the deck, at the scattered debris that was all that remained of his raft.

"What now?" he asked aloud, not expecting an answer.

***

Amy. God, where do I even start? I've been thinking about you a lot out here. Too much, probably. But what else is there to do when you're lost at sea, right?

I keep trying to figure out what we are—what we were. Was it love? Lust? Some fucked-up mix of the two? I don't know anymore. Maybe I never did.

You drove me crazy, you know that? Still do, even now. That wild energy of yours, the way you'd laugh at the dumbest jokes, how you'd drag me out of my comfort zone. It was intoxicating. Dangerous. I felt alive with you in a way I hadn't in years.

But it wasn't all sunshine and roses, was it? We fought like cats and dogs sometimes. You'd push and push until I snapped, then act all hurt when I did. It was exhausting. Exhilarating, but exhausting.

I told myself it was just physical at first. A fling, nothing more. But who was I kidding? You wormed your way under my skin, into my head. I started comparing Jennifer to you, finding her lacking in ways I never had before. It wasn't fair to her. It wasn't fair to any of us.

I think about that night on the beach sometimes. Remember? When we snuck out and ran down to the water like a couple of teenagers. You looked so beautiful in the moonlight, your hair all wild from the wind. I wanted to freeze that moment, to live in it forever.

But then morning came, and with it, reality. The guilt, the shame, the fear of getting caught. It always came crashing back.

I don't know if I ever really loved you, Amy. Not in the way you deserved, anyway. But I cared about you. More than I should have, more than I had any right to. You made me feel young again, reckless and free. But at what cost?

I'm sorry. For everything. For leading you on, for not being strong enough to end it sooner. For putting you in an impossible situation. You deserved better than to be someone's dirty little secret.

I'm sorry for what I did to you, Amy, to us. I'm so fucking sorry.

Nineteen

Pete's head throbbed as he stared at the journal entry. The words blurred and shifted and a memory crashed through his mental fog like a wave breaking against rocks. Amy. She had been here, on the boat. The realization hit him with physical force, leaving him breathless.

He saw her standing on the dock, blonde hair whipping in the sea breeze, just as he was about to cast off. That mischievous glint in her eye, that wild grin.

"Surprise, sailor," she'd called out. "Thought you could sneak off without me, huh?"

Panic had gripped him then. But Amy, in her typical fashion, laughed it off.

"Relax, Pete. I told everyone I was visiting my sister in St. Thomas. No one's gonna know."

He'd protested, of course. Weakly. But Amy had always had a way of wearing him down, of making his resolve crumble like sand castles in the tide.

"C'mon, doc," she'd teased, already climbing aboard. "Live a little."

The memories cascaded now. Amy sprawled on the deck, soaking up the sun. Amy leaning over the railing, pointing out shapes in the clouds. Amy pressing a cool metal object into his hand as the sun dipped below the horizon.

The flask!

His eyes snapped open, darting around the cabin until they landed on the silver container. He lunged for it, turning it over in his hands. There, etched into the bottom, were the initials he'd missed before: A.L.

"Amy Larson," he whispered, his throat tight.

He remembered now. She'd produced it from her bag with a flourish, proclaiming it was time to "make some memories." He had hesitated, but Amy's enthusiasm was infectious. Before long, they were passing the flask back and forth, laughing at nothing and everything.

But there was something else, wasn't there? He furrowed his brow, concentrating.

The sextant.

Of course. How could he have forgotten?

It had been a gift. A peace offering, maybe, or a bribe. Amy had presented it to him the morning they set sail, producing it from her oversized beach bag with a nervous smile.

"I found it in this little antique shop," she'd explained, watching anxiously as he turned it over in his hands. "The guy said it was authentic. From some old whaling ship or something. I thought… I don't know. I thought you might like it."

He had been touched, despite himself. It was a thoughtful gift, far more personal than the usual trinkets Amy tended to shower him with. He'd thanked her, genuinely grateful, and her face had lit up with relief and something that looked suspiciously like hope.

Now, he fumbled through the cabin, searching for the sextant. He found it tucked away in a drawer, gleaming dully in the dim light. He ran his fingers over the intricate brass work, marveling at the craftsmanship. How had he convinced himself this had always been on the boat?

The weight of it in his hands grounded him, anchoring him to reality in a way nothing else had since... since when? He realized with a start that he had no idea how long he'd been out here. Days? Weeks? It felt like an eternity.

He sank onto the bunk, the sextant cradled in his lap, as more memories washed over him. Amy, insisting on taking the wheel, her laughter carrying on the wind as she steered them further and further from shore. The two of them, huddled together in the cabin as a sudden squall rocked the boat. Her lips on his, tasting of salt and tequila and something dangerously like love.

And then... what? He strained, but everything after that was a blur of disjointed images and half-remembered sensations. The storm. The albatross. The whale. Had any of it been real? All of it? None of it?

One thing was clear: Amy had been here. She wasn't some phantom conjured by his guilt-ridden mind. She had been flesh and blood, real and warm and alive.

So where was she now?

He clutched the sextant, as the memory of their argument crashed over him like a wave. It had started innocently enough, as these things often do. They were lounging on the deck, basking in the afterglow of their lovemaking, when Amy had turned to him with those big green eyes of hers.

"Pete," she said, her voice soft but determined. "We need to talk about telling Jennifer."

He tensed immediately, his body going rigid.

"Amy, we've been over this."

"I know, I know," she sighed, sitting up and wrapping her arms around her knees. "But I can't keep living like this. Sneaking around, lying to everyone. It's eating me up inside."

He sat up too.

"It's not that simple."

"Why not?" Amy demanded, her voice rising. "You don't love her anymore. You've said it yourself."

"It's not about love," he snapped, instantly regretting his tone when he saw Amy flinch. He softened his voice. "It's about responsibility. Commitment. You wouldn't understand."

As soon as the words left his mouth, he knew he'd made a mistake. Amy's eyes flashed dangerously.

"I wouldn't understand?" she repeated, her voice low and dangerous. "What, because I'm just some flighty, dumbass blonde? Is that what you think of me, Pete?"

"No, that's not what I meant," he'd backpedaled, but it was too late. The dam had broken.

"Then what did you mean?" Amy demanded, standing up now, her hands on her hips. "Explain it to me, oh wise one. Explain why it's okay for you to cheat on your wife, to lie to her face every day, but it's not okay to be honest with her."

He had felt his temper rising to match hers.

"You think I enjoy this? You think I like sneaking around, feeling guilty all the time?"

"Then why do it? Why not just end it with her?"

"Because it's not that simple!" He exploded, jumping to his feet. "There's more at stake here than just my feelings, or yours. There's my practice to think about, my reputation—"

"Oh, your precious fucking reputation. God forbid anyone find out that the great Dr. Corbin is human like the rest of us."

"That's not fair."

"Isn't it? Face it, Pete. You're a coward. You want to have your cake and eat it too. Well, I'm done being your dirty little secret."

He'd staggered back, his face pale.

"What are you saying?" he said.

Amy had taken a deep breath, squaring her shoulders.

NINETEEN

"I'm saying that when we get back, I'm telling Jennifer everything. With or without you."

"You can't do that," he said, his voice hoarse.

"Watch me," Amy replied, her chin jutting out defiantly.

Pete had felt panic rising in his chest, threatening to choke him.

"Amy, please. Think about what you're saying. You'd ruin everything."

"Everything?" Amy repeated, her voice breaking. "Is that all I am to you? A threat to your perfect life?"

"No, of course not," he said, reaching for her. But Amy had stepped back, out of his reach.

"Don't," she said, her voice cold. "Just... don't."

They'd stood there, the silence between them as great as the Caribbean sea. He had opened his mouth, closed it again, at a loss for words.

Finally, Amy spoke, her voice barely above a whisper. "I love you, Pete. God help me, but I do. But I can't keep doing this. It's killing me."

He had felt something break inside him at those words. He'd wanted to tell her he loved her too, that he'd leave Jennifer, that they could start a new life together. But the words had stuck in his throat, held back by fear and guilt and a lifetime of playing it safe.

Instead, he said, "I need time. To figure things out. To find the right way to tell her."

Amy laughed, a bitter, hollow sound that had made his heart ache. "Time. Right. Because that's worked so well for us so far."

She'd turned away then, heading for the cabin. He called after her, but she'd ignored him, disappearing below deck.

The memory faded. He was alone in the present, clutching the sextant like a lifeline. He felt hollow, gutted. How had he forgotten all of this? How had he convinced himself he was alone on this boat? That he'd come on this trip alone?

And the question still stood, where was Amy now?

At that moment, he noticed something on one side of the sextant that he could swear was not there before.

Dried blood...

Pete's fingers trembled as he traced the pattern of dried blood on the sextant. The metal felt cold against his skin, but his mind burned with a sudden, searing heat. Images flashed before his eyes, vivid and horrifying, like a movie reel spinning out of control.

He saw Amy's face, contorted in anger and pain. He felt the weight of the sextant in his hand, saw it moving violently through the air. The sickening crunch as it connected with her skull. The look of shock and betrayal in her eyes as she collapsed to the deck.

His stomach lurched. He dropped the sextant, stumbling back until he hit the railing. His legs gave out, and he slid to the deck, his breathing erratic and heavy.

The memories kept coming, relentless and merciless.

Amy, sprawled on the deck, blood matting her blonde hair. Her lips moving, forming words he couldn't hear over the roaring in his ears. His own hands, reaching out, wrapping around her throat.

He looked down at his hands now, half-expecting to see blood. They were clean, but he could feel the phantom sensation of Amy's pulse beneath his fingers, growing weaker and weaker.

He remembered the panic that had gripped him, the desperate need to silence her. To stop her from telling Jennifer, from ruining everything he'd worked so hard to build.

The sound of her final, choked gasp echoed in his ears. The way her body had gone limp, her eyes staring blankly at the cabin ceiling.

He doubled over, retching. Nothing came up but bile, burning his throat.

When the heaving subsided, he sat back, his head spinning. The

NINETEEN

memory wasn't done with him yet.

He saw himself dragging Amy's lifeless body out of the cabin and across the deck, leaving a trail of blood that gleamed in the moonlight. The strain in his muscles as he lifted her, the sickening moment of weightlessness before he let her fall overboard.

The splash seemed to echo across the empty sea, accusing him.

He clutched his head, trying to block out the images, the sounds, the overwhelming guilt that threatened to drown him. But it was no use. The truth was out now, and there was no escaping it.

He had murdered Amy. In a moment of blind panic and rage, he had snuffed out her life and cast her into the sea like garbage.

A sob tore from his throat, raw and animalistic. He cried for Amy, for the life he had taken. He cried for himself, for the man he had become. He cried until he had no tears left, until his throat was raw and his eyes burned like hellfire.

As the storm of emotion passed, a terrible clarity settled over him. Everything made sense now. The hallucinations, the gaps in his memory, the inexplicable injuries. His mind had been trying to protect him from the truth, spinning elaborate fantasies to keep the *true* horror at bay.

But now the truth was out, and he knew there was no going back. He was a murderer. A monster. And no amount of rationalizing or self-delusion could change that fact.

He looked out at the sea, picturing Amy's lifeless, fish-eaten body out there somewhere, drifting in the currents. The thought made him sick all over again.

He closed his eyes, wishing he could wake up and find this all to be just another nightmare. But when he opened them again, nothing had changed. The boat was still damaged, the sextant still lay on the deck where he had dropped it, and the weight of his terrible deed still pressed down on him, threatening to crush him entirely.

***

I killed Amy, he scrawled, the words looking alien on the page.

God help me, I fucking killed her.

He hesitated, taking a shuddering breath before continuing.

I need to write this down. I need to remember. Maybe if I put it on paper, it'll stop playing over and over in my head.

Amy and I had been arguing. She wanted me to leave Jennifer, to tell her everything. Said she was tired of being the other woman, tired of sneaking around.

I told her she was crazy, that I couldn't just throw away my marriage, my practice. She got mad, really mad. Started yelling about how she was gonna tell Jennifer herself if I didn't.

I panicked. I couldn't let that happen. Everything I'd worked for would be gone. So I grabbed the sextant - the one Amy had given me as a gift, for Christ sake - and I hit her. Just once, but hard. Right on the side of her head.

She went down like a sack of potatoes. There was blood, so much blood. I thought she was dead right then, but she wasn't. She was looking up at me, her eyes all glassy and unfocused. She was trying to say something, but all that came out was this gurgling noise.

I don't know what came over me. It was like I was watching myself from outside my body. I knelt down next to her and put my hands around her throat. I squeezed and squeezed until she stopped moving. I couldn't just let her lie there and suffer like that. I had to finish it.

After that, I just sat there for a while, staring at her body. I couldn't believe what I'd done. But then I started thinking about what would happen if anyone found out. I'd go to jail. I'd lose everything.

NINETEEN

So I cleaned up as best I could. Wrapped her body in a tarp from the storage locker. It was heavy, dragging her across the deck. I almost lost my grip a couple times.

When I got to the railing, I hesitated. For a second, I thought about trying to revive her, about turning the boat around and getting help. But it was too late for that. So I pushed her over the side.

The splash when she hit the water...

After that, I guess I kind of lost it. Started seeing things, hearing things. My mind trying to protect me from what I'd done, I suppose.

But now I remember everything. Every detail. The way her eyes bulged as I choked her. The sticky feeling of her blood on my hands. The sound of her body hitting the water. All of it.

I'm a murderer. A godamm piece of shit murderer. What am I supposed to do now? How do I live with this?

I keep thinking about Jennifer. About my patients. What would they think if they knew? I'm supposed to help people, for fuck's sake. Instead, I killed a woman with my bare hands. A woman who loved me.

I don't know how to end this. I don't know if there's any way to make this right. Maybe I should just jump overboard myself, join Amy in the depths. But I'm too much of a coward for that. I admit it.

So here I am, adrift. A murderer, confessing to a journal that no one will ever read.

If there's a hell, I'm sure I've earned my place in it.

Twenty

The words Pete had written were a damning confession of his heinous act.

"What have I done?" he whispered.

The reality of his actions crashed over him like a wave, threatening to drown him in a sea of guilt and horror. He'd killed her. Murdered her in cold blood. A woman he'd claimed to care for, snuffed out by his own hands.

He stumbled to his feet, nearly tripping as he lurched across the cabin. His reflection in the small mirror stopped him cold. The face staring back was unrecognizable - hollow-eyed, wild-bearded, haunted.

"You're a monster," he told his reflection, voice cracking. "A fucking monster."

He sank to the floor, his back against the wall, and buried his face in his hands. Sobs wracked his body, deep, guttural sounds that seemed to come from the very depths of his soul. He cried for Amy, for the life he'd taken. He cried for Jennifer, for the trust he'd betrayed. He cried for himself, for the man he'd thought he was, now forever lost.

As he wept, memories of Amy flooded his mind. Her laugh, her smile, the way her eyes lit up when she talked about her dreams. All of it gone, extinguished.

"I'm sorry," he choked out between sobs. "God, I'm so sorry, Amy."

But sorry wasn't enough. Sorry wouldn't bring her back. Sorry

TWENTY

wouldn't undo the horror of what he'd done.

He tried to make sense of how he'd gotten to this point. He was a psychiatrist. He was supposed to help people, not harm them. How had he become this... thing?

He thought of his patients, the trust they placed in him. What would they think if they knew? The idea of facing them, of pretending to be a healer when his hands were stained with blood, made him physically ill.

He scrambled to his feet and barely made it to the small bathroom before he vomited, his body rejecting the awful truth along with the contents of his stomach. He retched until there was nothing left, then slumped against the cool porcelain.

As he sat there, shaking and sweating, a new thought occurred to him. What if he turned himself in? Confessed to the authorities, faced the consequences of his actions? It was the right thing to do, wasn't it?

But the idea of prison, of spending the rest of his life behind bars, filled him with a paralyzing fear. He wasn't built for that kind of life.

"Coward," he spat at himself. "You're nothing but a godamm coward."

He dragged himself back to his feet, splashing water on his face and stumbled back into the main cabin, his eyes falling on the journal where it lay on the table. The urge to destroy it, to rip out the pages and burn them, was almost overwhelming. But he couldn't bring himself to do it. It was evidence of his crime, yes, but it was also the only record of the truth. The only testament to Amy's fate.

He picked up the journal, clutching it to his chest as if it were a lifeline. In a way, it was. It was the only thing keeping him tethered to reality, preventing him from slipping back into the comforting delusions his mind had created.

"What do I do now?" he asked the empty cabin, his voice small and lost. "How do I live with this?"

He sank into a chair, the journal still pressed to his chest. He felt hollowed out, empty. The man he'd been before - Dr. Pete Corbin, respected psychiatrist, loving husband - that man was gone. In his place was this… this shell, this murderer.

He thought of Jennifer, of the life they'd built together. How could he ever face her again? How could he look into her eyes, knowing what he'd done? The idea of confessing to her was unbearable. She'd hate him, be disgusted by him. And rightly so.

His thoughts turned to his father, to the disappointment and disgust he'd surely feel if he knew what his son had become. All those years of trying to live up to his father's expectations, of trying to prove himself worthy, and now this. He'd become something far worse than anything his father had ever accused him of being.

The weight of his actions, of the life he'd taken and the lives he'd ruined, pressed down on him like a physical force. He felt crushed by it, suffocated. There was no way out, no way to make this right.

"I can't do this," he whispered, his voice breaking. "I can't live with this."

But even as the thought crossed his mind, he knew he couldn't do it. He was too much of a coward, too afraid of what might await him on the other side. So he sat there, paralyzed by guilt and fear, trapped in a hell of his own making.

His eyes darted to the window, drawn by a sudden movement. The albatross that had been haunting him for days, weeks, who knows how long, was there, its massive wings spread wide against the darkening sky. But as he watched, the bird's form began to shift and change.

Its feathers melted away, revealing pale skin. The beak softened into full lips. The wings morphed into slender arms. And then, impossibly, Amy was there, hovering outside the boat, her blonde hair flowing in the wind.

He stumbled back, his heart hammering.

TWENTY

"No. You're not real. You can't be real."

But Amy just smiled, that same impish grin she'd always had. She pressed a hand against the glass, and he could swear he felt the warmth of her touch.

His legs gave out. He squeezed his eyes shut, willing the apparition to disappear. But when he opened them again, she was still there, watching him.

"You're not here," he said, his voice shaking. "I... I killed you."

Amy's laugh was like wind chimes.

"Oh, Pete. You can't get rid of me that easily. We're connected, you and I. For better... or worse."

She drifted closer, her form passing through the glass as if it wasn't there. He pressed himself against the wall, trying to put distance between them.

"Why are you here?" he asked.

Amy cocked her head, studying him.

"Why do you think? You called me here, Pete. Your guilt, your fear... it's like a beacon."

She floated down until she was eye level with him, cross-legged in the air as if sitting on an invisible chair.

"Plus, I couldn't let you have all the fun out here by yourself, could I?"

Pete's laugh was more of a sob.

"Fun? This isn't fun. This is... this is hell."

"Is it?" She reached out, her fingers brushing his cheek. He flinched at the touch, cold as ice. "Or is it just what you deserve?"

He shook his head, trying to clear it. This wasn't real. It couldn't be real. And yet...

"I'm sorry," he blurted out. "God, Amy, I'm so sorry. I never meant to—"

"Shh," she interrupted, pressing a finger to his lips. "I know, Pete. I know you didn't mean it. But you did it all the same, didn't you?"

Her words were like a knife to his heart. He felt tears welling up in his eyes.

"I did," he whispered. "And I can't take it back. I can't fix it."

Amy's smile turned sad.

"No, you can't."

"I'm a murderer, Amy. A monster."

"You're human," she said. "Capable of terrible things."

She reached out again, this time taking his hand in hers. Her touch was still cold, but there was a strange comfort in it.

"You have a choice now, Pete."

He looked at her, really looked at her. She seemed so real, so present. Part of him wanted to believe this was really Amy, that she had somehow forgiven him. But the rational part of his mind knew better.

"You're not real," he said again, but this time with less conviction. "You're just... you're just my guilt talking."

Amy shrugged.

"Maybe. Or maybe I'm something more. Does it really matter?"

She floated back a bit, her form starting to blur around the edges.

"What matters is what you do now, Pete. How you choose to deal with what you've done."

He felt panic rising in his chest as she began to fade.

"Wait!" he cried out. "Don't go. Please, I... I don't know what to do."

Amy's smile was the last thing to fade.

"Yes, you do," her voice echoed. "You just have to be brave enough to do it."

And then she was gone, leaving him alone once more with his thoughts and his guilt.

TWENTY

* * *

To whoever finds this - if anyone ever does - I need you to understand.

I don't know why I did it. I keep trying to understand, to rationalize it somehow. Was it the alcohol? The stress? The fear of being caught? Or was it something darker, something that's always been inside me, just waiting for the right moment to come out?

But in the end, none of that matters, does it? One moment of madness, and I'm a murderer. A monster.

Jennifer, if you're reading this, I'm sorry. I'm sorry for betraying you, for lying to you, for not being the man you thought I was. You deserved better than me. You always did.

Dad, I know you always thought I was weak. Guess you were right, huh? Your son, the coward. The killer.

To Amy's family, I don't expect you to forgive me. I don't want you to. What I did is unforgivable. But I need you to know that Amy was special. She was bright, and funny, and full of life. And I snuffed that life out. I'll never forgive myself for that.

I keep seeing her face. Not just in the moment I... in that moment, but all the times before. Her smile, her laugh, the way her eyes lit up when she talked about her dreams. And now she'll never get to fulfill those dreams. Because she met... me.

I don't know what happens after we die. As a doctor, I've always dealt in the realm of the physical, the provable. But out here, lost at sea, haunted by ghosts, I'm not so sure anymore. If there is something after, I hope Amy's at peace. And I hope that someday, somehow, she can forgive me.

If your'e reading this, I beg you - learn from my mistakes. Don't let fear and selfishness drive you to do terrible things. Don't throw away everything good in your life for a moment's weakness.

I don't know how much longer I'll last out here. Part of me hopes I'll be *rescued, that I'll have to face the consequences of what I've done. But another part... another part hopes the sea will claim me, the way it claimed Amy. Maybe that's the only way to balance the scales.*

I'm sorry. I'm so, so sorry. For everything.

Twenty one

Pete stared as water slowly began filling the boat. It crept in with an almost living quality, inch by relentless inch. He wondered idly how long it would take before the Harbinger was completely submerged. Hours, maybe. He found he didn't much care anymore.

He leaned back against the cabin wall, feeling the gentle sway beneath him. The sun painted the sky in brilliant oranges and purples as it descended toward the horizon. He thought it might be the most beautiful sunset he'd ever seen. Funny how things like that seemed to matter now.

"I deserve this," he said aloud.

The albatross - or was it Amy's spirit? He couldn't tell anymore - remained overhead, silent and watchful. He raised a hand in a mock salute.

"You win. You can stop haunting me now. I'm done."

He closed his eyes, letting the sounds of the sea wash over him. The waves against the hull. The distant cry of seabirds. The creaking of the boat as it settled lower in the water. In these final moments, he found an unexpected peace.

His thoughts drifted to Jennifer, to the life they'd built together. Was she worried about him? Angry? Or had she already guessed the truth somehow? He hoped she'd be okay, that she'd find someone who deserved her.

The water reached his ankles, cold and insistent. He remained still, accepting its advance, feeling the weight of his guilt pressing down on him like a physical thing.

Night fell gradually, stars appearing one by one. He watched them emerge, trying to remember the constellations his father had taught him as a boy. Orion's Belt. The Big Dipper. Cassiopeia.

The water rose to his waist, soaking through his clothes. Its chill penetrated deeper than he'd expected, but he welcomed the discomfort. This was his penance, his judgment. He deserved to feel every moment of it.

He closed his eyes again, letting his head fall back against the cabin wall. The exhaustion of weeks - or had it been months? - settled into his bones. He was tired of running, tired of lying, tired of pretending to be something he wasn't. The world would be better off without Dr. Pete Corbin, the fraud, the adulterer, the murderer.

The water continued its relentless rise, patient and inevitable. He didn't fight it. He sat motionless, feeling the cold seep into his core, listening to the dying sounds of his boat.

He thought about writing one last entry in his journal, but what remained to say? He'd confessed his crimes, begged for forgiveness he knew he didn't deserve. The story was complete.

So instead, he waited. It seemed fitting somehow. A kind of cosmic justice.

As the water reached his chest, he found himself oddly calm. The fear and panic he'd expected never materialized. Instead, there was only acceptance. This was how it ended. This was what he'd brought upon himself.

* * *

TWENTY ONE

The water had stopped rising. It lapped gently at his chest, but no longer creeping higher. Pete sat there for a long moment, confused, waiting for the inevitable to continue. But nothing happened.

Finally, with a groan, he pushed himself to his feet. Water cascaded off him, sloshing around the cabin. He stumbled, grabbing onto the edge of a nearby shelf to steady himself. His legs felt weak, unsteady after sitting for so long.

His eyes fell on the radio. It sat there on the shelf, miraculously dry. He stared at it, a war raging in his mind. Part of him wanted to just sit back down, to let the sea take him as he'd planned. But another part, a part he thought he'd silenced, whispered of hope.

He reached for the radio. It felt heavy in his grip, weighted with possibility and dread. His finger hovered over the call button.

"What the hell," he muttered. "Might as well go out with the truth."

He pressed the button, hearing the familiar crackle of static.

"Mayday, mayday. This is the Harbinger. Can anyone hear me?"

He waited, listening to the hiss of dead air. He was about to try again when a voice crackled through, faint but unmistakable.

"This is Coast Guard Station Saint Croix. We read you, Harbinger. What's your situation?"

He let out a bitter laugh.

"My situation?"

He breathed in deeply.

"I've done something terrible. I... killed someone. A woman. Her name was Amy Larson."

The words hung in the air, heavy and irrevocable. He waited for a response. When none came, he continued, the words spilling out of him like the water from his sinking boat.

"She was my girlfriend. We had an argument. I hit her with a sextant, then I... strangled her. Pushed her overboard."

He paused, swallowing hard.

Static crackled, then the voice returned.

"Sir, can you give us your location?"

"I have no idea. I've been lost for weeks, maybe. I don't even know anymore."

He looked around the waterlogged cabin, at the wreckage of his life.

"The boat's taking on water. I thought… I thought I was going to die out here. Maybe I should."

"Sir, we're going to do everything we can to find you. Can you describe any landmarks you can see?"

He moved to the cabin door, pushing it open. The albatross was still there, wheeling overhead against the night sky.

"There's nothing," he said. "Just water and stars. And this damn bird that won't leave me alone."

He turned back to the radio.

"Listen, I need you to understand. I'm a murderer. I killed Amy, and I've been lying to my wife for months. I don't deserve to be saved."

"Sir, that's not for us to decide. We're here to help. Can you tell me about your boat? Any distinguishing features that might help us spot you?"

He closed his eyes, feeling the weight of his guilt pressing down on him.

"It's a Grand Banks Classic Trawler. Forty-three footer. Burgundy and black hull, cream deck. The name's on both sides - Harbinger."

He paused, then added, "Fitting name, isn't it? I should have known it was an omen."

"Okay, that's good information. Can you tell me about your supplies? How much food and water do you have left?"

He glanced around the cabin.

"Not much. A few cans of food, maybe a day's worth of water. I wasn't planning on needing it for long."

He sank down onto a bench, the radio clutched in his hands like a

TWENTY ONE

lifeline.

"I don't know what to do," he admitted, his voice breaking. "I thought I had it all figured out. I was going to let the sea take me, pay for what I'd done. But now…"

"Now you have a chance to face what you've done," the voice on the radio said gently. "To take responsibility the right way."

He nodded, even though he knew they couldn't see him.

"Yeah. Yeah, I guess so."

Pete lowered the radio, his hands shaking. The confession had left him drained, hollow. He closed his eyes, trying to steady his breathing.

"Well, well, well. Look who finally decided to come clean."

His eyes snapped open. There, perched on the edge of the navigation table, was Jennifer. His wife. She looked exactly as she had the day he left - hair pulled back in a neat ponytail, arms crossed over her chest, one eyebrow raised in that infuriatingly knowing way of hers.

"Jenny?" he whispered. "How are you here."

She rolled her eyes.

"Maybe I'm just another figment of your guilty conscience. Like the bird, like the whale, like poor, dead Amy. Or… maybe I'm *more* than that. Maybe we *all* are."

He flinched at Amy's name.

"I didn't mean to—"

"Oh, spare me," Jennifer cut him off. "You didn't mean to what? Cheat on your wife? Murder your mistress? Abandon your patients? Which part exactly didn't you mean to do, Pete?"

She hopped off the table, moving towards him with fluid grace. He stumbled backwards.

"I'm sorry," he mumbled. "God… Jenny."

"Sorry doesn't cut it, Pete. Sorry doesn't bring Amy back. Sorry doesn't undo months of lies."

She was right in front of him now, her hazel eyes boring into his. He could smell her perfume - the same scent she'd worn on their wedding day. It made his chest ache.

"What do you want from me?" he asked, his voice barely above a whisper.

Jennifer's face softened for a moment, and she reached out as if to touch his cheek. But her hand passed right through him, and he felt nothing but a cold shiver.

"I want you to face what you've done," she said. "All of it. No more running, no more hiding in a bottle or behind your work or out here on this godforsaken boat."

He slid down the wall, sitting in the shallow water that still covered the cabin floor. Jennifer crouched in front of him, her expression a mix of pity and disgust.

"You know, I always wondered if you'd cheat," she said conversationally. "You had plenty of opportunities - all those conferences, late nights at the office. But I trusted you. I thought, 'Not my Pete. He'd never do that to me.'"

She laughed, a bitter sound that made him wince.

"Guess I was wrong about that, huh?"

"It wasn't… it wasn't like that," he tried to explain. "Amy, she was…"

"She was what?" Jennifer snapped. "Young? Exciting? Not worn down by years of dealing with your bullshit?"

He shook his head.

"No, it's not… I don't know why I did it. I just… I felt trapped. Like I couldn't breathe."

Jennifer stood up, towering over him.

"And now? How's the breathing now, Pete? Out here in all this open air, with Amy's body somewhere at the bottom of the ocean?"

He buried his face in his hands.

"Stop it," he said. "Please, just stop."

TWENTY ONE

But Jennifer wasn't done. She paced the small cabin, her movements jerky and unnatural.

"You know what the worst part is?" she said. "It's not even the cheating. It's the lying. All those nights you came home late, all those weekends you said you were fishing... You looked me in the eye and lied, over and over and over again."

She stopped, fixing him with a stare that seemed to pierce right through him.

"How long were you planning to keep it up? How long before you slipped up, before I found out? Or were you just going to leave me? Run off with Amy and start a new life?"

He looked up at her, his eyes red-rimmed.

"I don't know. I hadn't thought that far ahead. I just... I was just trying to get through each day."

Jennifer laughed again, that same harsh sound.

"Well, congratulations. You made it through to this day. The day you confessed to being a murderer on an open radio channel. The day you finally ran out of lies."

She crouched down again, her face inches from his.

"So what now, Pete? What's your grand plan?"

He shook his head.

"I don't have one," he whispered. "I thought... I'd die out here. That it would be easier that way."

"Easier for who? For you? What about Amy's family? What about me? Did you think about us at all?"

He felt tears stinging his eyes.

"I'm sorry," he said again, knowing how inadequate it was. "I'm so, so sorry."

Jennifer stood up, her expression hardening.

"It's time to face the music. Time to be the man I thought I married."

With that, she vanished. He sat there for a long time.

Finally, he reached for his journal... one last time.

* * *

This is my final entry.

My name is Dr. Pete Corbin, and I am - was - a psychiatrist in Frederiksted, St. Croix, U.S. Virgin Islands. I'm writing this from my boat, the Harbinger, somewhere on the Caribbean Sea. I don't know how long I've been out here. Weeks maybe. Time has become... fluid.

I came out here to escape, to find some peace. Instead, I found only madness and death. I've done terrible things. Unforgivable things. I cheated on my wife, Jennifer, with a woman named Amy. And then... God help me, I killed Amy. I killed her and threw her body overboard like she was nothing.

I've been haunted by what I've done. By Amy's ghost, by visions of my wife, by an albatross that seemed to follow me everywhere. I don't know what was real and what wasn't anymore. Maybe none of it was real. Maybe all of it was.

To whoever finds this boat, this journal: Please make sure it gets to the proper authorities. Let the truth be known, let closure be had.

As for me... I don't know what comes next. The boat is half sunken. I could try to save myself, to radio for help again. But I don't think I deserve to be saved. Not after what I've done.

So this is goodbye. To the world, to my life, to everything I've known and loved and destroyed. I don't ask for understanding or sympathy. I only ask that the truth be told.

May God have mercy on my soul.

Dr. Pete Corbin

He closed the journal and placed it carefully on top of the desk, where

TWENTY ONE

it would be easily found. Then he stood up, water sloshing around his legs, and made his way to the deck.

The albatross was there above him, as always. He looked up at it, wondering if it would follow him to whatever came next.

He filled his lungs with the salty sea air. For a moment, he thought he heard Jennifer's voice on the wind, calling his name. But when he turned, there was nothing.

He was tired, so tired. Of running, of hiding, of fighting against the inevitable.

He looked out at the horizon, where the sky met the sea in a seamless line. Somewhere out there, beyond his sight, was home. Was Jennifer. Was the life he'd left behind.

Twenty Two

The albatross, Pete's constant companion, transformed right in front of him. Its wingspan stretched impossibly wide, body swelling until it rivaled a small dragon. Its eyes blazed like twin flames against the darkening sky.

Each pass brought it lower, the wind from its wings whipping across the deck. Pete's heart hammered in his chest as the massive creature dove, passing inches above his head. He scrambled across the wet deck, losing his footing.

The bird wheeled for another attack. This time, its talons raked across Pete's back, tearing cloth and flesh. Pain blazed across his skin.

"Stop!" he screamed, but his voice was lost in the thunder of wings.

The attacks came relentlessly. He swung wildly, trying to defend himself, but it was like fighting smoke. Blood trickled down his face, filled his mouth with copper.

He lunged for the cabin door, desperate for shelter. Before he could reach it, talons seized his shoulders, piercing muscle and scraping bone. His feet left the deck as the bird lifted him skyward.

The Harbinger shrank below, becoming a toy boat in a vast bathtub. His stomach lurched as he watched his last connection to safety disappear.

"Please," he whimpered, though he wasn't sure what he was begging for.

TWENTY TWO

Then the talons released him.

For one crystalline moment, Pete felt weightless, almost peaceful. Then gravity claimed him, and he plummeted toward the waiting sea. The impact drove the air from his lungs, stunning him…

And then the vision shattered.

Pete found himself standing at the edge of the Harbinger, toes curled over the gunwale. For the first time in what felt like an eternity, his mind was clear. The constant chatter of guilt and fear had fallen silent, leaving only profound calm.

He closed his eyes, remembering Amy's face - not the twisted, accusing specter that had haunted him, but the real Amy. The woman he'd destroyed.

When he opened his eyes again, the sun was just breaching the horizon, painting the world in gold. Beautiful. Perfect.

He took one deep breath, held it, then let it go. With it went years of pretense, of lies, of trying to be something he wasn't. With calm acceptance, he stepped off the boat.

The water shocked him with its cold embrace. For a moment, instinct took control and he thrashed against the sea's pull. Then he stopped, surrendering to its depths.

As he sank, a strange peace enveloped him. The initial cold faded to numbness. He opened his eyes, watching his final breath escape in silver bubbles that danced toward the surface, growing smaller until they vanished entirely.

The underwater world held an otherworldly beauty. Shafts of morning sunlight pierced the depths like golden spears. Schools of tiny fish darted past, scales glinting like scattered coins.

His lungs began to burn, but he made no move to save himself. He let the weight of his clothes pull him deeper into the blue abyss. The sea had been his escape for so long - now it would be his final resting place.

His mind drifted as his body sank. He thought of Jennifer, her practical nature that had both anchored and frustrated him. Their first date, his nervous laughter, her patient smile. The life they'd built, the dreams they'd shared. Sadness washed over him as he realized he'd never get to apologize for all the ways he'd failed her.

Then Amy filled his thoughts. Sweet, impulsive Amy, who'd brought such passion and chaos into his life. Her laugh, her wild spirit, the way she'd made him feel alive again. The memory of her body sinking into these same waters flashed through his mind.

As oxygen deprivation took hold, his thoughts fragmented. Childhood memories surfaced - rare moments of connection with his father, his mother's fierce pride at his medical school graduation, her crushing embrace.

The pressure in his chest became unbearable, but still he made no move to swim. This was right. This was justice. For Amy, for Jennifer, for everyone he'd hurt along the way.

Consciousness began to fade, the edges of his vision darkening. A profound peace settled over him. The guilt, the fear, the self-hatred - all of it melted away, leaving only quiet acceptance. He'd made his choices, and now he faced their consequences.

The world grew darker, reality bled away. His final coherent thought was of the albatross, that haunting presence that had guided him to this moment.

As the last bubbles escaped his lips, Pete Corbin closed his eyes and surrendered to the sea.

Epilogue

The U.S. Coast Guard Investigator, Officer Allison Quint, sat in the cabin of the half-sunken Harbinger, Pete Corbin's journal in her hands. The last entry burned in her mind - a cold farewell from a man who'd lost himself at sea. She blinked, trying to process the darkness she'd uncovered.

The overturned furniture and scattered belongings told a different story now. What she'd initially cataloged as evidence of a struggle now spoke of a man's descent into madness.

Her investigation had started routinely enough - a distress call, a confession of murder, a search and rescue operation. Instead, she'd found a tale that challenged everything she thought she knew about human nature.

The beginning of Pete's journal had seemed ordinary: a successful doctor taking a fishing trip to clear his head. The gradual unraveling of his psyche, documented in increasingly erratic entries, had drawn her in like an undertow.

The crackle of her radio shattered the silence.

"Officer Quint, come in. Over."

"This is Quint. Go ahead."

A pause stretched across the airwaves.

"We've got an update on the Corbin case. Jennifer Corbin was just found dead in their basement. Apparent strangulation. Over."

The words struck Allison hard. Her hand tightened on the journal until her knuckles went white.

"Repeat that last, over." Her voice sounded distant to her own ears.

"Jennifer Corbin is dead. Found in the basement of the Corbin residence. Preliminary cause of death appears to be strangulation. Local PD is on scene now. Over."

Allison stared at the journal, its pages heavy with unspoken horrors. The final entries, filled with guilt and self-loathing, took on a darker significance.

"Copy that," she managed.

She set the radio down with mechanical precision. Her mind raced through the journal's contents, searching for clues she might have missed. Phone calls with Jennifer, arguments - had they been real, or delusions? Where did Pete's madness end and reality begin?

She pushed herself up, needing to move. Her eyes swept the cabin again - the empty flask, the antique sextant, the meticulously stored fishing gear that stood in stark contrast to the surrounding chaos. Each item held a piece of the story, but how many pieces was she still missing?

The weight of it pressed down on her. A respected psychiatrist with a perfect life, harboring such darkness. A wife murdered in her basement. A mistress somewhere in the depths of the Caribbean. Three lives destroyed, and she was left to piece together why.

Allison braced herself against the cabin wall, forcing herself to breathe steadily. She was a professional. She had a job to do.

With methodical precision, she began gathering evidence. The journal, of course. The sextant. Anything that might illuminate the truth of what had happened on this boat, in that basement, in Pete Corbin's fractured mind.

She couldn't shake the feeling that she was only scratching the surface. The line between guilt and madness, between reality and delusion, had

EPILOGUE

never seemed so thin.

The Caribbean stretched around her, a graveyard for Pete's secrets. Somewhere in its depths, his body drifted and so did the remains of Amy Larson. And back in Frederiksted, Jennifer Corbin's body waited, the final piece of this tragic puzzle.

Allison squared her shoulders. There would be questions to answer, reports to file, a case to build. But she knew the story of Pete Corbin would stay with her, a reminder of how easily a life could unravel when pulled by the right threads.

As she prepared to leave the Harbinger, a piercing screech split the air. She tilted her head skyward, squinting against the harsh sun.

There, hovering overhead, was an unusually large albatross.

About the Author

Rowan Duncan (b. 1977) is an American writer from West Texas. His writing explores themes like Nature, Existentialism, and the darker aspects of Human Nature.

His range of genres includes Crime, Neo-Noir, Neo-Western, Thriller, Horror, Southern Gothic, and others. Literary influences include Edgar Allan Poe, Arthur Conan Doyle, Ernest Hemingway, J.D. Salinger, Stephen King, and Cormac McCarthy.

He began writing at the age of fifteen after winning a short story contest put on by his 8th grade English teacher. It was his very first time writing anything fictional.

Contact Rowan at: RowanDuncanWriting@gmail.com

You can connect with me on:
- https://author-rowanduncan.com
- https://x.com/RowanDuncan_1
- https://www.facebook.com/rowan.duncan.author

Also by Rowan Duncan

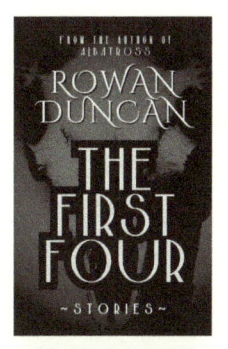

The First Four
A collection of the first four stories written by Rowan Duncan. These tales deal with the darker aspects of human nature, delving into subjects like murder, crime, violence, guilt, loss, and grief. But there is also redemption, forgiveness, and justice.

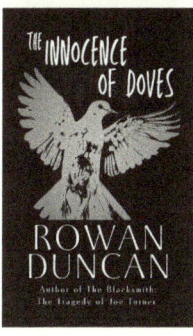

The Innocence of Doves
The Maclane family has worked their ranch for generations, their roots as deep as the ancient oaks that dot their land. But when a shadow falls across their homestead, they'll need more than grit to survive.